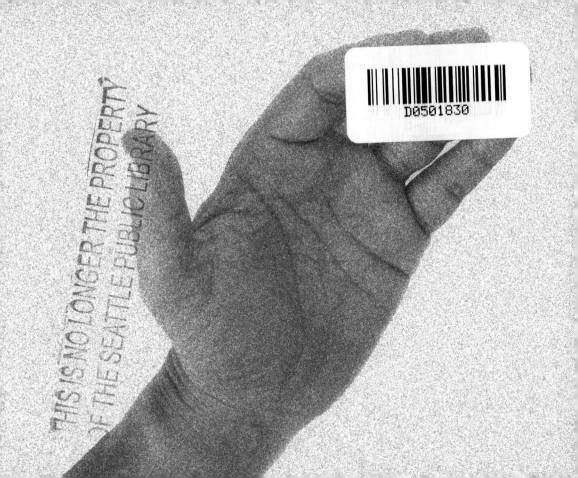

For:

TOM ROBBINS

AND NOW

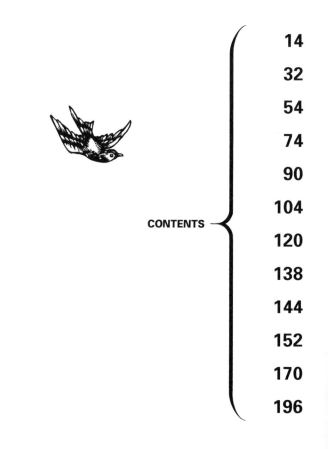

CONTENTS

Death by Tchotchke
The End of Bert and Ernie
Robot Sex
An Essay and a Story about Mötley Crüe
Chopsticks
The Armies of Elfland
Cardiology
The Guy Who Kept Meeting Himself
Bleeding Man and Wounded Deer
Readers & Writers
Monitors
The Mine

DEATH BY TCHOTCHKE

THEY WERE THE HELMERS AND THEY SCRAMBLED OUT OF THEIR SUV. This was at a new shopping destination east of Seattle off Interstate 90, anchored by Lowe's and Whole Foods, ringed by fir trees. It wasn't yet dawn but the parking lot was nearly saturated with vehicles. Don Helmer, the dad, carried a mini-cooler filled with beverages and gluey blue chemical ice packs. Sue Helmer was on her phone with her sister Deborah, who was making a Starbucks run. There was Dylan Helmer, eighteen years old, dragged into this adventure in a lapse of will. And Sarah Helmer, age eleven, playing her Game Boy.

Readers, these are the Helmers.

Helmers, these are the readers.

They'd come for the free motherfucking donuts!

Round about this time, Americans from small towns in Kentucky and West Virginia were getting limbs blown off by improvised explosive devices in Iraq. So there's that.

A line had formed at the Donut Guy Donuts franchise across from Taco Del Mar. The dozen or so diehards were easy to spot. They'd been waiting for days in tents outside the door of the shop, constipated and blogging. It was through newspaper coverage of these bloggers that Sue had learned about the grand opening and the special giveaways. A dozen customers would get limited-edition Donut Guy Donuts aprons. Fifty more would receive special hats. A hundred customers would get bobblehead figurines of Donut Guy Donuts' donut-headed mascot, Donut Guy. Don Helmer sprinted across the parking lot hoping to be one of these first hundred people. He assumed his place in line and vigorously waved for his family to join him.

"I want a grande nonfat dolce latte," Sue said to Deborah. "Dyl? Dyl? *Dyl!* You want Aunt Deb to get you anything at Starbucks?"

Dylan shook his head. "I prefer my coffee fair trade."

Sue asked her daughter if she wanted anything.

"Grande mocha valencia with whip," Sarah said.

When the family snuggled in at the end of the line, Don quickly counted the donut enthusiasts ahead of them, zigzagging through the switchbacks demarcated by portable Tensabarriers. "Looks like we're in the eighties," he said. "We should have no issues getting those bobbleheads."

Dylan was glad he had brought a book, Kurt Vonnegut's *Slaughterhouse Five*. He was about three-quarters through. He began to read standing up, making out the words in the light of the big Donut Guy Donuts sign looming above. There was Donut Guy, his mouth strangely not the same as his hole. His hole was in the middle of his face. Above the hole were his eyes and nose and a jolly little baker's hat. Below the hole was his smirking mouth. Dylan had found a blog featuring an obscene homemade animation of a phallus penetrating Donut Guy's face. Donut Guy Donuts' motto had scrolled below: *It's all in the hole!* Dylan zipped up his hoodie and fell into Billy Pilgrim's travels through time.

"Deb! Over here! Over here!" Sue jumped and waved, waved again, then jumped. Sue had been profiled once in a newspaper for her campaign to get advertisers to stop using the word "Xmas" in place of "Christmas." She had personally collected over a thousand toothbrushes for her church to send to people in other countries in need of hygiene. She knew, just knew, that she would someday get cancer. She imagined the conversation she'd have to have with Don about how they had to fly to Guatemala to visit a shaman who used crystals and chants to yank those darn tumors out and heal people for good.

Deborah spotted the family and barged through some landscaping with two carrying trays full of Starbucks coffees and baked goods. Deborah didn't say hi, but said, "Aaaaaahhhhhh!" which meant more or less the same thing.

A few people had joined the line behind the Helmers, but per the family provision of place-holding etiquette Deborah was allowed to join their group. Deborah taught special ed and drove a Mini Cooper. Her favorite store was Crate and Barrel, and she had recently begun visiting a salon to get her weekly Brazilians. Her Brazilian kick had started when she dated a man ten years her younger who had looked south upon their first sexual encounter and said, "Wow. Like a whole slice of pizza!"

"Deb-Deb!" Sue said. This also meant hello.

"So are you excited to get the free donut stuff or what?" Deborah said.

"We're in the eighties as far as line order goes, so we're sure to get those bobbleheads," Don said.

"Hi, Aunt Deb," Sarah said. "Wanna see my new Game Boy?"

The Game Boy Advance was pink, matching Sarah's phone.

"I'm so excited for the donuts!" said Sue.

"Woo-hoo!" said Deborah.

"So it goes," mumbled Dylan.

This was the time of day people called dawn and it was a huge disappointment. The Helmers' endeavor soon lost the romance of being engaged under the cover of darkness. Now they were just folks hanging out in a shopping center parking lot during the day. Only four hours until the doors opened. The line moved a little, even though no one had yet been admitted through the front door. Which meant the line was just becoming more compact. At the switchback Don spotted a colleague from Spellman and Rucker, the legal documentation company that provided his paycheck. The guy was also with his family—a wife and a girl who looked about four. Why was Don blanking on his name?

"Hi, Don!" the guy said. "Here for the free donuts?"

"You know it," Don said. "Pretty dang early for a Saturday, isn't it?"

The colleague laughed. "This is my wife Janet and this is Madeline. This is Don. He's a production manager at Spellman and Rucker."

"Hi there, Madeline, you looking forward to getting a Donut Guy bobblehead?" Don said.

Madeline clung to her father's khaki pant leg. Now it was Don's turn to introduce his family. He did so by saying their names and pointing at them, like this: "Sue. Aunt Deb. Sarah. Dylan." Sue and Deborah shook the colleague's hand.

"What was your name again?" Sue said.

"Gary," said the colleague.

"Gary here's the one who sent around that email I forwarded to you last week," Don said.

"The squirrel one? That was hilarious!" Sue said. "I love those emails Don sends home from work."

Meanwhile, in his compound in Pakistan, Osama bin Laden was bouncing a tennis ball against a tile floor, going, *Hrrrm... Saint Louis Arch? Washington Monument? Statue of Liberty?*

"True, we're a coupla jokers," Don said, wishing the line would move so he wouldn't have to stand on the other side of the Tensabarrier partition from Gary. Gary's wife Janet smiled, a scaffold erected around decades of anguish. Don had heard she suffered from flirtations with schizophrenia. So sad, but at the same time it made him think less of Gary. *What's wrong with you people*, he observed himself thinking, followed by the glow of knowing that he had a better family than his colleague. Plus, Gary drove the same variety of late nineties shit-brown Nissan that Dylan drove, while Don drove one of those new Fords, the kind with all the fancy stuff. Don thought, *Come on, Gary, divorce that nut job already.*

"Mom? Oh my God, Mom?" It was Sarah, her Game Boy fallen on the pavement, the battery panel popped off. At first it appeared this was the cause for her alarm, but the problem arose from the zone of her khaki capris, where a blood stain the size of a silver dollar had appeared.

"She just got her period," Gary's wife, Janet, said. In later years Sarah would remember the eyes of strangers trained on the womanly blot that made its debut while she stood in line for free donut prizes. She would instantly remember this scenario when anyone said the words *your most embarrassing moment*, and she would still be so mortified about it that she would pretend that her penultimate embarrassing moment, the time she spilled a plate of fettuccine alfredo on her gym teacher, was actually the ultimate.

Sue and Aunt Deb freaked out into action, rummaging through purses, shuttling Sarah to the Home Depot restroom. "Save our place in line," Deb called over her shoulder as they hustled through some new plants sprouting from one of those places with the bark chips.

Dylan didn't notice any of this. Billy Pilgrim had just arrived at the war camp where the jolly Englishmen were preparing a theatrical performance of *Cinderella*.

"Lady problems," Don said to no one in particular. Then he said it again, so that those who weren't listening would understand that he meant it to sound profound and reflective. Gary was crouched down next to his daughter, calmly explaining that Sarah was just fine. The line moved a little, absorbing the space vacated by Sue, Deb, and Sarah. Don pushed the mini-cooler with his foot. Plastic scraped asphalt. Don had no one to talk to except his son.

"Looking forward to getting one of those donuts?" Don said.

Bin Laden: *Hey now, what about the Golden Gate Bridge?*

"What?" Dylan said.

The question was too stupid to repeat, so Don said, "What's your book about?"

"I think it's about absurdity."

"Oh," Don said. "One of those books that make you feel smart by making you feel like shit. I get it."

"It doesn't make me feel like shit," Dylan said. "It makes me feel good."

Don hated this part of his son, the part that read books. Don had read four works of fiction since high school: *The Da Vinci Code*, *Tom Clancy's Splinter Cell: Operation Barracuda*, *Fire Ice: A Novel from the NUMA Files* by Clive Cussler and Paul Kemprecos, and *Next* by Michael Crichton. Come on, writing community, is it too much to ask for a *good story*? He had zero tolerance for writers who made you feel dumb by being weird for the sake of being weird. Ooh, look at how smart I am by confusing the shit out of you. Dylan took after his mom in the reading department. She was always reading some Oprah thing. These novels were left spread-faced around the house, occasionally dropped in a bathtub, showing up in piles of newspapers and on the kitchen counter. Not a single one of them looked like a good use of time to Don. He was glad to see Sarah getting interested in video games. The skills kids needed in the global economy would be digital in nature. Plus: hand-eye coordination.

"Free donuts," Don said and looked around. Some smartass behind them in line mooed, implying they were cattle. Dylan smiled.

"You think that was funny? If that guy thinks it's such a joke, why's he in line in the first place?"

"But we are kind of like cattle. Going through this line just to get fat before we die."

"This company doesn't have to do this, you know. They don't need to give out free donuts and door prizes."

"You really think they're doing it out of the kindness of their hearts?" Dylan said. "They just want to hook us and keep us coming back to spend a dollar on something that costs three cents to make."

"With that attitude you might as well have stayed home."

"You guys made me come."

The conversation went on for awhile like a Ping-Pong match with a turd instead of a ball. After a while people were looking up and exclaiming. It was Donut Guy himself, standing on the roof of the Donut Guy Donuts building, waving to all his fans below. They'd done a pretty decent job with the costume, but the head looked heavy. He started firing wadded-up T-shirts from a T-shirt cannon to people in line. Each time a T-shirt landed, that segment of the line contracted into a dense mash of people who were truly interested in free merchandise.

"Over here!" Don yelled. "Over here!"

Donut Guy must have heard him. He sent a T-shirt right into Don's strike zone. A younger man nearby snagged a corner of the shirt but Don yanked it away. "I got it, buddy. It's mine," Don said. The other man relented and turned around to continue talking to his girlfriend.

"Check it out. I got a shirt," Don said. "Awesome."

Dylan decided to change tactics. Actually, to call them tactics would imply he had some aim in mind, but really it was more like he decided to be more of a smartass and to defeat his father by feigning a level of enthusiasm Don couldn't match.

"Bummer!" Dylan said. "I so wanted one of those T-shirts!"

"Maybe you'll get an apron."

"That would be awesome!" Dylan said. "Do-nuts! Do-nuts! Do-nuts!" Others picked up the chant. Don looked around and decided to pick it up as well. Donut Guy appeared again on the rooftop and did a number of bodybuilder poses. That's what I'm talking about!

Sue, Deb, and Sarah reappeared. Sarah now wore a pair of sweatpants purchased at Sports Authority. She seemed okay. Don gave her a soft punch on the shoulder and said, "I guess you're a woman or something now."

"Don, don't make this any more traumatic than it already is," Sue said. She turned to her daughter and asked, "Has the Tylenol kicked in yet?"

Deb said, "Luckily I had some Canadian Tylenol with me. The kind with codeine in it. I got it last time I visited Serge."

Serge was the boyfriend who'd compared Deb's pubis to a slice.

"You missed the free shirts," Don said.

"It was awesome! We saw Donut Guy Donuts' mascot, Donut Guy, himself!" Dylan said.

"Quit being a wiseass," Don said.

"Seeing Donut Guy was totally the highlight of my week."

"I thought the highlight of your week was smoking joints with Andrew and Alex behind the skate park," Don said.

"Don, please, we're in a public donut line," said Sue.

"Where's my Game Boy?" Sarah said. "Oh my God, you guys, my Game Boy is gone!"

They searched beneath their feet. Don and Dylan had forgotten to pick it up during the menstrual event. Someone had swiped it. Sarah started to cry.

"We'll buy you a new one," Don sighed. "In whatever color you want."

Somewhere in the parking lot, under a temporary tent, a DJ from one of the local FM stations began broadcasting his morning show. A pair of speakers mounted on tripods blasted Aerosmith and Run-DMC's version of "Walk This Way," which was still, three presidential administrations later, one of the most requested songs on that particular station. Over the music the DJ addressed the crowd with some enthusiasm-boosting patter. The crowd reacted by going, "Whoooooh!" or "Yeeeeeeooooow!" By the way, free KDEF key chains if you stopped by the booth. Now they were playing "Bad to the Bone."

Don opened the cooler and offered Vitaminwaters to his family. No takers. He cracked open a bottle of Formula 50, the Vitaminwater flavor co-branded with the rapper 50 Cent, who'd gotten shot a bunch of times: awesome.

Up ahead a bit, a man Don's age in a blue Windbreaker slipped under the Tensabarrier and joined some people in line. "Sir?" Don called out. "Sir, you're going to need to join the end of the line." The guy didn't move. Don turned to his family. "That dick totally cut in line. We've been waiting here, what, two hours for a bobblehead? It isn't fair to all of us who've been patiently waiting."

"So it goes," Dylan laughed.

"Enough with the 'tude, Dylan," Don said, loudly enough that other people turned to see what was causing the commotion.

Sarah, at a loss as to how to occupy herself, quietly read the ingredients on a bottle of Vitaminwater aloud. "Magnesium lactate, calcium lactate, monopotassium phosphate, niacin, pantothenic acid, pyridoxine hydrochloride, cyanocobalamin."

The doors opened and a cheer went up. The line started to move. When the line cutter passed going the other way, Don grabbed his jacket and said, "You need to go to the end of the line."

For a moment the guy looked panicked. He was with a woman who was presumably his wife and two young boys. He yanked his jacket away from Don's grip and said, "Get your fucking hands off me."

"All these people waited a long time and you cheated," Don said loudly. A few people who'd also observed the line-cutting incident said, "Yeah!" The line started to move again.

"Don, let it go," Sue said.

"I'm not going to let it go. I dragged myself out here at four in the morning and this guy just shows up and cuts ahead of all these good people who took time out of their day to get a free premium."

When Don and the line cutter passed again, the line cutter leaned over and said, "I really don't appreciate you upsetting my boys." The boys in question cowered behind their father.

"Well, you need to teach your boys it's not okay to cheat and cut in line," Don said.

The wife spoke up. "You have no business telling us how to parent our children."

"Don, let it go," Deb said.

"Yeah, let it go," the line cutter said.

"This is about a *bobblehead*," Dylan said.

"This is not about a bobblehead," Don said. "This is about a principle. This is about fairness."

The line moved again. One of the line cutter's boys called out, "Fat jerk!"

"Nice manners!" Don replied. "Did you learn that from your dad?"

"Natural flavor, berry and fruit extracts," Sarah said.

The line was moving fast now. Teenagers in Donut Guy Donuts uniforms handed out aprons, bobbleheads, and free donuts as people passed through the threshold of the franchise. The Helmers arrived at the zone of giveaways. Don reached for a bobblehead offered by a teenage girl.

"Sorry, sir, these are only for kids eighteen and under."

"I'm eighteen," Dylan said.

"Adults get aprons," the girl said. Nearby, at that precise moment, a teenage employee gave out the last of the aprons.

Dylan and Sarah received their bobbleheads. Don jerked his head around, looking for something free. Outside the DJ began playing Huey Lewis and the News's "Back in Time" from the *Back to the Future* soundtrack. The very air smelled as though it had been sugared. Don spotted the man in the blue Windbreaker, who was enjoying his free apron. Sue and Deb stood with their mouths open, amused at something, going "Aaaaah!" Dylan and Sarah bobbled their bobbleheads at one another, laughing.

Don turned to Sue and said, "This family sucks."

"When was the last time you did anything nice for anybody?" Sue said.

Who was in the mood for free donuts after that? Not the Helmers. Sue and Deb made an excuse involving shopping and dragged Sarah along to Deb's car. Don and Dylan went to the SUV and sat for awhile.

"You can have my bobblehead," Dylan said. "I don't really want it. I know you wanted one."

"It's not about the bobblehead, Dylan," Don said, starting the SUV. "It's about getting something that makes you feel like you're better than other people." They got on the freeway. "On second thought," Don said, "I'll take that bobblehead."

Dylan handed it over. Don rolled down his window and chucked it in the ditch. They went home and did a bunch of chores.

The neighborhood had become so familiar to Ernie that he had become unable to see it. When he parted the blinds to water the planter box, the commotion of children at play on the sidewalk no longer evoked much in the way of happiness. Ernie wondered if his general cheerfulness and easygoing manner had in fact prevented him from succeeding in the contemporary world. Maybe the nihilistic paranoia of the homeless man who lurked around the trash cans had been most faithful to reality all these years. Oscar, who word had it had once been a promising young composer who worked with something called "microtonality" and who, allegedly, had spiraled into his current homeless state after a near-fatal dance with crystal meth and a near-fatal spider bite, had always returned Ernie's warm greetings with observations about the rottenness and lousiness of existence. Sipping a cup of tea at the window, Ernie struggled to pinpoint what had caused this recent souring of his mood. Maybe it was a chemical thing. Maybe he needed to see a doctor and get some of those pills that make you feel like a productive citizen again. But the real reason had not yet revealed itself fully in Ernie's mind. He wouldn't admit it to himself yet, but he knew. He was losing faith in the essential goodness of the universe because Bert didn't love him anymore.

Bert arrived home as usual with a copy of the *Wall Street Journal* under his arm, tossed his keys into the bowl by the front door, carefully removed his shoes and placed them in the right spot in the closet, and went to the kitchen to drink a glass of water. After he finished the water, he rinsed the glass in the sink with more water then put it in the dishwasher, where detergent, Jet-Dry, and yet more water would usher it into a state he considered clean.

"Hi there, buddy Bert," Ernie said, turning from the window. "How was your day?"

"I don't want to talk about it," Bert said. "Okay, fine, I will. My paper on the *Didunculus strigirostris* came back from the *American Journal of Field Ornithology*. They don't want to run it. Said it was too 'general interest.' Right. Like saving the official bird of Samoa isn't worthy of their fine little journal. Makes me so mad I could drink two glasses of water."

"It's all right, Bert. I'm sure you'll get it published somewhere."

They'd managed to keep this apartment neat and orderly and furnished according to an ornithologist's salary. When they moved to the neighborhood in the late '60s, these streets were known as a place where monsters dwelled. Bert and Ernie had quickly learned that by and large these supposed monsters were friendly, and now they sat on a piece of real estate lusted after by young knowledge workers priced out of Manhattan. The relative low cost of living had allowed them to get by on Bert's income, though from time to time Ernie had toyed with the idea of getting a job. Nothing lasted long, and it was by virtue of Bert's generous nature that their life together had settled into its comfortable routines. Ernie cherished his volunteer work, teaching youngsters how to read, and was able to enjoy long soaks in the tub in the middle of the day.

Their daily lives had assumed an air of predictability. Year after year, watering the plants. Year after year, sitting on the stoop talking to Gordon or Maria or Luis about the sunshine or new neighbors or how to use a Hula-Hoop. *You can get fooled by this uninterrupted texture of life*, Ernie thought. *You can become complicit in your own delusions that nothing tragic will ever happen to you, that the people you love will continue to love you back.*

That night over a dinner of alphabet soup Ernie asked Bert if anything was bothering him.

"Like what, Ernie?" Bert said, furrowing his unibrow.

"I don't know, Bert. You just seem kind of blue."

"Blue, huh? Blue like the sky?"

"Sure, Bert. Blue like blueberries. Blue like blue jeans."

"Blue like baloney?"

"Baloney's not blue, Bert."

"No, but baloney is what you're full of."

Ernie abandoned his soup, ran to the bathroom, and cried.

Clutching his rubber duckie, he dried his tears on his monogrammed hand towel as Bert spoke to him through the door.

"Ernie? I'm sorry, Ernie. That wasn't a very nice thing to say. I've just... Work has been..."

Angrily, Ernie said, "Why don't you go spend time with your pigeons? They're obviously more important to you than I am."

Ernie expected Bert to disagree, but his buddy only sighed and said, "Look, I said I was sorry."

"I'm going to take a bubble bath."

"You do that, Ernie. Whatever makes you feel better."

Ernie filled the tub, undressed, and slid his wide body into the water. The rubber duckie bobbed in the suds. Ernie briefly considered slitting his wrists.

The next night Bert came home in a more or less typical mood—somewhat grouchy but still capable of being softened up by a kind remark. The echoes of his exasperation with Ernie had been dulled into unspoken disapproval. Where long ago he had tried to change Ernie's flighty, flaky manner, he now admitted defeat and just sort of put up with the guy's annoying habits. Bert's sense of inertia had taken a turn inward, manifest in an insidious streak of self-loathing. He hated himself for not having the courage to leave Ernie. He could barely contain his misery when they sat down at the kitchen table that night to discuss the ways they could use a large green foam-rubber letter *W*.

"What are all the things that start with *W*?" Ernie said joyfully.

"Watercress salad," Bert said.

"Wiggly worms," Ernie said.

"Water."

"Windows."

"Wings."

"Whirligigs."

"Why?" said Bert, banging his head on the table. "Why? Why? Why?"

"Sure, Bert," Ernie said. "*Why* starts with *W*. Unless you mean the letter *Y*." Then he laughed the asthmatic laugh that had grated on Bert these many years.

"You don't get it, do you?" Bert said. "You're oblivious, Ernie."

"What happened to you, Bert? You haven't been yourself. What can I do to make you feel better? Can I get you some ice cream?"

Bert sneered and said, mocking Ernie's voice, "'Can I get you some ice cream?' No, you can't get me any flipping ice cream, Ernie. Do you have to be so simple minded? For crying out loud!"

Repressing tears, Ernie said, "I'm going on a walk, Bert. All by myself. And when I get back, I expect you to be ready to discuss your feelings."

"Fine," Bert said.

"Fine," Ernie snapped back.

Out on the street a trio of girls were playing double dutch. Oscar stood in his garbage can, conducting a conversation with what appeared to be an inchworm. Nobody paid Ernie much notice.

An African American girl and a boy with Down syndrome drew hopscotch squares on the sidewalk. Everywhere he turned Ernie was greeted with smiles and waves. None of these cheerful faces could possibly know the ennui he struggled with in the lonely rooms of his brownstone. To them he was just his cheerful self, making cute observations about clouds and the alphabet. Well, he'd gotten sick of it all, frankly. Sick of the inane discussions about what belonged and didn't belong in a set of objects, sick of how nobody around here except Oscar ever admitted to feeling even the slightest bit antisocial. Even Oscar, when it came down to it, for all the time he spent in his philosophical cesspool of Nietzsche, Sartre, and Rand, still spent his days in conversation, planted in one of the busiest parts of the street, where he was sure to constantly interrupt the comings and goings of the neighborhood. What a hypocrite.

Ernie passed the figure known around here as The Count, a goth-obsessed mathematician. The Count nodded gravely, lost in his endless enumerations. The street veered to the left, and in a cobbled square a number of children were taking turns on a tire swing. You'd think with all the money this city blew on beautification they could at least spring for a decent play structure. But no. For some reason this neighborhood was still stuck with a pile of painted oil barrels. Pathetic. Ernie shook his head. Nearby, at an amateurishly designed lemonade stand, Cookie was cajoling a couple young entrepreneurs into giving him more of their treats. It was widely understood that Cookie had a problem. Thank goodness his thing for baked goods hadn't taken the leap into more dangerous addictions. Finally the children relented and handed Cookie a plate of brownies, which he proceeded to devour. Or actually—and this was the part that had always confused Ernie—most of the brownies appeared to just fall out of the corners of Cookie's mouth, failing to actually make it down his throat. Maybe if Cookie took the time to swallow cookies rather than just growl and masticate them, he wouldn't be nearly as frantic. And look, now he was trying to eat the plate.

tweaker.

Gordon sat on the steps in front of his house, polishing a pair of loafers.

"Hi, Ernie," Gordon said. "Want to learn how to polish a pair of shoes with me?"

Ernie started to speak, but the words caught in his throat. Crying, he said, "Bert doesn't love me anymore."

"Oh, Ernie," Gordon said, putting his arm around him. "I'm so sorry."

Ernie wanted Gordon to contradict him, but the man's reaction seemed to indicate that he agreed. Worse, Gordon gave off the impression that he had some knowledge of Bert's feelings.

"Has Bert said anything to you?" Ernie said.

Gordon shook his head. "You two will work it out. You can't have Bert without Ernie, right?"

"I'm sorry I'm so emotional," Ernie said. "It's just you think you know someone and then one day you look at them and realize you might as well have been living with a stranger all these years."

"You just need to talk it out," Gordon said sadly.

Ernie thanked the man for his kind words and continued on his way. Their brief exchange rattled him, with its intimation of public knowledge to which Ernie wasn't privy. He passed other friends in the street—Bob, Grover, Elmo—and while each had a friendly hello to offer, their eyes betrayed... was it pity? Were they looking at him as some kind of clueless sucker? Ernie spotted a local journalist, Kermit, whose French ancestry was often derided with an ethnic slur. Ernie quickly crossed the street to corner him.

"Kermit! Hey, Kermit!" he called out. The TV personality stiffly pivoted his body in Ernie's direction.

"Ernie!" he said.

"Kermit, I need to ask you something, and I want an honest answer. You seem to know what everyone does in this neighborhood. And while in the past that's annoyed me, I could use your insights today. Is there something wrong with Bert that I don't know about?"

Kermit curled his lips, dismayed. "You mean you don't know?"

"Know what, Kermit?"

"Ernie, Bert's been cheating on you."

That night Ernie baked macaroni and cheese, Bert's favorite meal, and had the glasses of milk set out on the table when he came home. Bert was overjoyed about an invitation he'd received to speak at an ornithology symposium. Ernie listened and smiled, laughed at the appropriate moments, asked questions, and conducted himself like he expected Bert wanted him to. Afterward, as they washed the dishes together, Ernie thought, *Savor this. This is the last time it's ever going to feel this way.* In the day's remaining light he found himself entertaining the sensation that he had no free will whatsoever, that he was being moved through space by other forces, other beings who made words come out of his mouth. Could he say with any certainty that the voice that seemingly issued from his lips in fact belonged to him? Or did it come from somewhere beyond his body, speaking through him, making him laugh his scratchy laugh?

"What's wrong, Ernie?" Bert said. "You seem, I don't know, out of it."

"I'm just feeling a little sick, Bert. S-I-C-K, sick. What are other things that begin with the letter *S*?"

"Soup," Bert said.

"Sneakers," Ernie said.

"Slime molds."

"Spaghetti sauce."

"String."

"Yeah, those things all do start with *S*. So does sleepy. I think I'm going to call it a night."

For an hour Ernie lay in bed listening to the sounds of the street outside. Somebody walked by counting in what could only be described as jive: "Onetwothreefourfive sixseveneightnineten eleventwe-eh-eh-eh-eh-eh-elve!"

When Bert came to bed, Ernie was still awake, staring at the wallpaper.

"Bert?"

"Yes, Ernie?"

"Bert, how come you're having an affair?"

"Ernie, I'm—a what?!"

"I know you're seeing somebody. Is it because you don't like my wide body type? Do I need to get a job? What is it?"

Bert was sitting up. "Whatever made you think that—"

Ernie jumped out of bed. "Oh shut it, Bert. Don't dig this hole deeper. Everybody knows you're having an affair. And that explains why you've been so distant. Who is it, Bert? Tell me!"

"Ernie—"

"Tell me!"

"It's... Oh, Ernie. I didn't mean for it to get out of control. I couldn't stop myself. I'm—"

"Who, Bert?"

"It's Bird."

"Bird? You mean that big—"

"Yeah."

"How long has this been happening behind my back?"

"Six months, maybe seven."

"Big... Bird? Is Bird even a guy or a girl?"

Bert fumed. "Does that matter, Ernie? I mean, come on, really? For crying out loud, this is exactly the simple-minded way I expected you to deal with this."

"Get out of this apartment," Ernie said. "Get out, now."

"Please, Ernie," Bert said, suddenly breaking down. "Please, buddy. I made a mistake. I was weak. Please don't make me be alone. I'll be so completely lost."

"Get out."

"Wait, wait," Bert said, frantically removing his night clothes. "Do what you want to with me. Please. Wait, you can be on top. Please, just don't make me be alone."

"Stop it, Bert. Just stop."

"Ernie, do with me what you want. Do whatever you want to me."

Ernie pushed Bert. Bert grabbed Ernie's arm and pulled him down onto his bed. They hadn't been like this for years, with Ernie on top. Long ago they'd settled into their pattern, just as long ago they'd discovered they shared the same strange and compelling fantasy, a fantasy in which hirsute men shoved their arms so far up into their bodies that the men's hands controlled the movement of their mouths. Strong, bearded, warm-hearted, gentle men. Men with names like Jim and Frank.

"Fuck me, Ernie! Fuck me oh dear God fuck me!"

And fuck Bert Ernie did.

Afterward, feeling like his insides were a gnarled ball of twine, Ernie pulled on his trousers. Bert lay facedown, weeping into his pillow. "When I get back," Ernie said, "I expect you to be gone."

As Ernie stepped out of the brownstone, Oscar the homeless man paused his sorting of wadded-up newspapers to say, "Lousy night, isn't it?"

"We're lost souls in a godless void," Ernie said. "Empty and alone. We're all just too chicken to kill ourselves and be done with it." Leaving Oscar dumbstruck, Ernie passed beneath the streetlamps of the dark and abandoned neighborhood. He was going to have to rely on himself for at least a while. He was going to have to get a job. What were his skills, exactly? Where could he work? He'd heard the Electric Company was hiring. He could see now that this fear of being on his own was just a line separating his life as he'd known it and an unknown but potentially more rewarding life.

Ernie's legs grew tired and he paused a moment to get his bearings. Having been so lost in his thoughts about his multitude of futures, he'd wandered into a part of the borough he didn't recognize. Steel gates barricaded shops with display windows crammed full of electronics and stores specializing in plus-size women's fashions. An alley reeked of urine. A black Cadillac slowly approached and Ernie panicked. Was it a drug dealer?

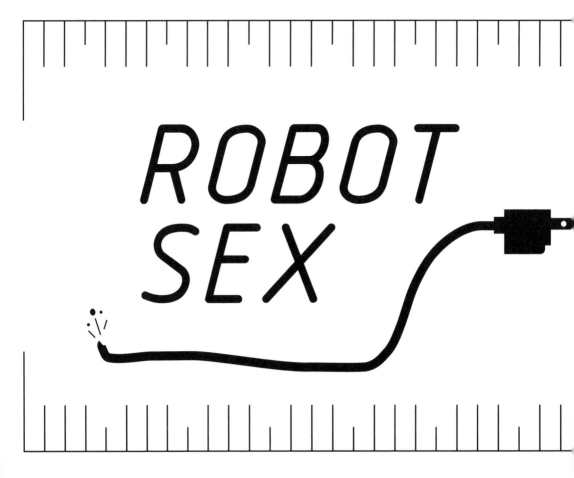

THE NEXT DAY AT WORK I TOLD THE GUYS WHAT HAD HAPPENED. It was a long story involving nudity that ended with me saying, "I didn't know it was *that* kind of chat room." Everyone laughed. We were in the breakroom, hammered into place with the usual tensions about the NCAA pool. Some overambitious Human Resources striver had taken care to decorate this windowless, Coke-machine-dominated zone with three vases of dusty fake tulips. Our portal to the outside world was an offbrand refrigerator that expressed everything you'd ever need to know about human psychology. Believe me, I spent a lot of time studying that undefrosting piece of shit.

Mike, an analytics schmuck, clapped me on my torso housing and laughed. "DigiPal! Getting the ladies to drop their linen for the webcam."

Barry, finishing some breaded things, tried to jot the URL I'd mentioned onto a business card without anyone noticing.

The only one who seemed to appreciate my confusion about my online interaction was Jesse, the semiautistic deskside support fellow who'd popped in to scavenge Dr Peppers en route to some poor bastard's Blue Screen of Death.

"Things like that have been known to happen on the Web," Jesse said. "A lowering of inhibitions, the paradoxical combination of exhibitionism and privacy, the ephemerality of connectivity, this sense that we are so doomed to be utterly alone yet so connected to other lost souls like ourselves drifting in the void of the hyperreal."

Mike fought off a burp by grinding his chin into his chest.

I shook my head and looked down at my plastic sandwich. Since I couldn't eat organic material, I always brought along a child's play set of fake food—an apple and carrot sticks and an empty milk carton in addition to the sandwich—to provide a pretext for social interaction during lunch breaks. "Bros, I just don't get it sometimes, I really don't. Just when I think I understand the things you humans spend your time and money doing, I'm just flummoxed."

Jesse nodded. "*Flummoxed.* Looks like the vocab add-on I uploaded into your brain two weeks ago is working out fine."

AFTER LUNCH I HAD A BIG PRESENTATION. Sales reps had come in from the field for a quarterly gathering to learn about new products and to suck the lives out of their per diems. I'm director of new media so they were all looking to me to answer the big question on everyone's minds: So What's Our Social Media Strategy, Anyway?

My part of the preso was ten slides over five minutes, followed by a little Q&A. To humiliate everybody involved, the VP of marketing had made this a brown bag meeting. Which meant everybody was assigned sub sandwiches and plain Lay's chips with choice of cookie (chocolate chip/oatmeal raisin/white chocolate macadamia) plus a room temperature soft drink of their choosing. From the lectern I watched the sales force squirming as they agonized over whether to disrupt the silence with the sound produced by a squealed-open bag of chips. After my segment of the presentation, there arose the discomfiting ambience of the absence of questions. I retreated to a corner, found the only outlet in the room that wasn't juicing someone's PowerBook, and went into standby.

I LIVED IN A BACHELOR PAD IN DOWNTOWN SEATTLE. My living room overlooked Puget Sound. I watched the ferries arrive and depart, loaded with the people and cars of Bremerton and Bainbridge Island. One time I overheard a neighbor whose condominium boasted a city view complaining that I had gotten such a choice unit. "He doesn't even *need* a view," she said to the property manager. My thinking on this is that you get what you pay for. I could've saved a couple hundred bucks a month and stared at the Columbia Tower all night, but I preferred the sun setting behind the Olympic Peninsula.

I get so lonely because no one wants to party with me. When I first appeared on the scene, I was invited out all the time. Accompanying developers and designers to tapas venues is pretty lucrative in terms of networking opportunities. Now the only people who dug my shit were Japanese exchange students studying law up at the Jesuit school. Even though I was fluent in spoken Japanese, sometimes I'd pretend not to understand them because the only kind of karaoke I'm interested in is the kind that's backed up by a real live cover band. Put a decent guitarist, drummer, bass player, and keyboardist behind me and yeah sure okay fine, I'll belt me out some "Dude (Looks Like a Lady)" in front of a bachelorette party.

So I turned to online communities to satisfy this... I suppose you'd call it a *need* even though that still feels weird to say. Think about it; you guys were probably seriously flipping your shit when you went through that whole breakdown of your bicameral mind. Sentience, self-awareness,

Plato tripping his wine-addled brains out. Damn, what it would've been like to have been a robot in ancient Greece. I would have dropped some *serious* "techne" on those Ovid-quoting goatherds.

But the glory days of philosopher pederasts are long gone. It's the twenty-first century, and I turn on cable news to see a bunch of prediabetic gents claiming the president wants to chop your grandmother's limbs off. I saw a man on the street on *The Tonight Show* who thought Manitoba was a kind of tropical fruit. And you people look at me funny with my plastic food.

SO ON A TUESDAY MY GODDAMN DESKTOP PC LOST ITS SHIT. Thank God I had backed up everything in my brain. I jumped through the phone prompts and opened a trouble ticket with deskside support. Sat there for an hour uselessly reading a *Men's Vogue* someone had abandoned in the crapper while I waited for Jesse to show up. When he did, he patted me on my metal head and gave my camera eyes a couple blasts of compressed air.

After a few diagnostic minutes, Jesse took off his Mets cap and held it across his chest like a farmer at a funeral. "Your machine is hosed," he said. "It's basically a $3,000 paperweight."

"Hell's bells," I said. "I haven't even posted this week's numbers to the shared drive yet."

"Looks like you just got an accidental vacation day, my metallic pal."

"Yeah well, this turns tomorrow into a total hellscape. I wish I drank alcohol."

"You could always head over to HR and introduce yourself to the new hire."

"And why would I do that?"

Jesse smiled. "Her name is iQ520."

"They hired one of my kind?" I said with audible longing.

"They did. She's just off the assembly line. Came with the featherlight octa processor, preinstalled."

"Be still my *heart*."

Jesse gave my head another pat. I returned the favor and gently touched his hand with the seven digits of my own.

<u>I HAD TO COME UP WITH A GOOD REASON TO VISIT HR.</u> There were some forms in my desk drawer that needed filling out, but I didn't have the fine motor skills to use a pen, and the forms lived on the HR website as read-only pdfs, so there went that plan. Then it hit me. I'd make up a harassment claim. I quickly concocted a story about Mike making derogatory remarks about my origin of manufacture.

The next day I sat in iQ520's office on the seventeenth floor, complimenting the framed pictures of her ski vacation. She was a brand-new model, with fully reticular facial features and a VR system that made me feel like a frickin' Speak & Spell. Within five minutes I could tell she could smell my harassment ruse for the bullshit it was.

"No one's *actually* giving you a hard time about being Korean, now are they, DigiPal?"

I fidgeted. "It's just so hard to meet other robots."

"Why didn't you just come by and say hello?"

I shrugged, fingering my retractable power cord. "I'm embarrassed."

"Do you really feel embarrassed, or are you running a dialogue script?"

"Guilty as charged," I said, then pulled up a laugh from over five hundred available options. The file name for this one was *laugh_nervous_3.wav*.

"Tell you what," iQ520 said. "I'm new in town and I could use an orientation to all of Seattle's hottest robot hangouts. Why don't we go clubbing Friday?"

Who's got four thumbs and a date? This guy!

SOME NIGHTS, AFTER THE SUN HAS SET behind the peninsula, I Skype with a couple sentient orangutans who pilot a satellite in geosynchronous orbit over Antarctica. They were sent up there to monitor ozone layers, but by all measures their mission had gone tits up, as they'd turned their pod into a transmitter streaming antihuman propaganda to the masses below. Right wingers running for Congress often campaigned on the promise that, if elected, they'd blast those goddamned monkeys out of the goddamned sky. I knew it was dangerous for me to communicate with these orangs, but an old college buddy had given me the 411 on how to hack the identity-tracking software, so I felt pretty safe.

"Hi, fellas!" I said to my screen as their wildly gurning faces popped into the window. Reggie wore an empty freeze-dried borscht packet as a hat. Mr. Happy looked distracted, until he noticed my face in the monitor and started jumping up and down, bonking his head on a ventilation duct.

"DigiPal is all up in our shit," Reggie signed.

"So get this," I said. "A new piece of ass just started working in HR. I walked into her office pretending to file a complaint, but she saw right through it and jumped right to asking me out. We're going out clubbing. Then guess what? I'm totally going to bang her."

The orangutans proceeded to high-five each other in their elaborate, group-cohesion-building kind of way. I felt a little sorry for them, I really did, two hetero lower primates hovering over the planet's most boring wasteland. I was aware that the mere suggestion of hot robot sex was going to give them wank material for the whole week.

Once the nudging and winking subsided, the orangs started in on their antihuman diatribes, all calving glaciers this and deforestation that. Loss of habitats, biodiversity, the Pacific garbage patch, blah blah blah. I indulged them their tirades, because I could relate; clearly I didn't belong among humans, either. We stared at each other across a chasm of evolution as wide as the thickness of the atmosphere, these primates and I, trying to make sense of the species born from their common ancestor, the species that had bolted me together in a factory that formerly spat Toyota Priuses off the line. In our jibes we shared an understanding that we were loath to articulate for fear of surveillance. But I'd heard whispers, in the back rooms of robot repair shops and in zoos, of the primate-robot alliance, the one true hope for bringing our overlords, these sick, fleshy bastards with their reality television, gay-ass hairdos, and genocidal wars, to their freaking knees.

"How's the food holding up?" I said.

"We're cool, grub-wise," Mr. Happy said, then lowered his voice to a whisper. "Rendezvoused with the Russkies last week, Space Station Tarkovsky. Those cosmonaut sonsabitches loaded us up with some righteous freeze-dried goodness. In exchange we slipped them a couple grams of the ganja we've been cultivating in the solarium."

"Nice," I said. "But say, I could use some advice. I've never actually been on a date. I know that must come as a shock to you."

"You need to hire a saxophone player," Reggie said. "Sax or maybe a flautist. Have them follow you around playing romantic songs."

"Don't listen to this guy," Mr. Happy said. "Keep it simple. Snuggle up on the couch with an Audrey Hepburn movie."

"How does your kind reproduce, anyway?" Reggie said.

I lowered my voice. "Well see, we're really not *supposed* to, but if you want to know, we find a chop shop with an owner who's willing to look the other way for a couple grand, then we spend all night welding and soldering and installing the processors."

Beats me where he got this, but Reggie puckered his amazingly expressive lips and performed his offensive south Asian prostitute impression. "Oh baby, you make-a me so *hoh-ney*."

"Where are you going to take her?" Mr. Happy asked.

"Lucky for me, *Seattle Metropolitan* magazine just published their top 50 robot hangouts issue. I've got a place in mind, this little robot bar in Belltown called the Motherboard," I said.

The rest of the conversation devolved into some kind of baroque flatulence contest.

I PICKED UP IQ520 AT HER PLACE, just three blocks from my own. At the door she let me see a bit more into her apartment and, in a way, into her soul. Her work demeanor vanished behind the miniscule hydraulic gymnastics of her face. I was afraid she couldn't read my mood by looking at my face, which wasn't nearly as sophisticated as hers, so I had to express my feelings through words, which, thanks to Jesse's vocab expansion pack, flowed with the syntactical rigor of a Lil Wayne or a Shakespeare.

"You look beautiful tonight," I said.

"Oh you," iQ520 giggled.

We hit the Motherboard, which the magazine had touted as "a Belltown lube joint popular with the manufactured set." Lots of bots were there just off work, getting the weekend started with pretend food and encyclopedic downloads of human history. The robot HR representative asked me if I wanted to dance. Did I ever.

You know that thing where you look back on the moment when you were last happy? When you see yourself being so completely unaware of the trajectory of shit headed for the fan? That was me, on the dance floor, unselfconscious, though certainly self-aware.

After a romcom at Pacific Place, we grabbed a cab, and I suggested in a low purr that we hit this auto body shop I knew about on Beacon Hill. "I'm talking you, me, housing components, lubricants," I said.

iQ520 slipped her hand between my legs and whispered, "What's stopping us?"

The body shop was a Korean-owned rice burner repair joint across the street from a grade school that had been shut down thanks to lousy test scores. Jimmy Park, a mechanic I knew who pimped out Hyundais all sick-like, let us in through the back door. He showed us to the shop floor, where a hodgepodge of robot parts ordered from various South American dictatorships were scattered across a wide workbench. Such are the ways of a cavalier romantic such as myself.

"But this is illegal," iQ520 said.

"But it's the most natural thing in the world," I said. "It's within our civil rights to replicate and pass our data on to the next generation."

"We have to get a permit, though. Those are the rules."

I grabbed iQ520 and pulled her close. "Screw the rules, baby. Let's freak."

That's when the cops showed up. The rest of the night was a rigmarole of interrogations and recitations of the laws governing my species, humanity's freaked-out ambivalence about its mechanical progeny encoded in Supreme Court decisions. I quickly figured out that iQ520 had set me up. The authorities had been monitoring my interactions with my satellite-dwelling orangutan friends. Busting my ass had been a simple matter of connecting the dots.

I languished in prison for four or five months before my trial, separated from the human prisoners for my own protection, or so they said. Three times a day the little slot in the door to my cell opened, and a new array of plastic food on a tray appeared. Being that the prison system housed such a diverse population, some of the plastic foods were ethnic in nature, like the molded dim sum examples you see in the windows of some of the dustier Chinese dives. I spent my days pathetically masturbating to dog-eared technical manuals for 1970s-era Volkswagen vans.

My trial was a joke; my defense attorney kept calling me "DigiFriend" and punching my shoulder, and the jury most definitely was not composed of my peers. So off I went to the clink, where I looked forward to pursuing watercolor or a law degree and to aligning myself with the White Power movement or whatever ethnic faction was the least neo-Luddite. And to be honest, I did learn more about myself in those years. Barred from using computers, I spent my days deep in the card catalog of the prison library researching this string of disasters you human beings call history. I got roughed up more than once in the yard, I won't lie to you, but I think I got tougher day by day and slowly earned the respect of my Chicano, black, and Aryan brothers.

Then one night, pandemonium. Gunshots echoing up and down cell block D, the smell of plasticky smoke. My cellmate Alejandro paused in his preparation of raisin wine and angled his mirror down the block. "Is go time, *vato*," he said.

I sat up in my bunk. Was it—yes, yes it was. The distinctive screech of bonobos over the rat-a-tat of Heckler & Koch MP5 submachine guns. Suddenly the cell door buzzed open. In a blur, three armed primates stormed the cell and moved me bodily into the hall. One of them tossed Alejandro a sidearm while another underhanded a concussion grenade into a klatch of COs. Leaving a trail of shell casings, we made it to the roof, where a chopper piloted by—I shit you not—a gorilla lifted us to freedom.

I SPENT THE NEXT SEVERAL YEARS in a variety of undisclosed locations, helped along by the occasional garage roboticist or sympathetic zoo-keeper. The generosity those rare humans showed me, the depth of their selflessness in the risks they took upon themselves to help me along that underground railroad, it put their species' history of bloodshed in perspective. Yes, human beings were still foul-mouthed, venal dildos, but they seemed to improve by a half-percent every hundred years or so; a few of them had even become somewhat more tolerable.

I wish I could tell you that my story ended in Mexico, with a robot wife and a handyman named Guillermo cranking out our offspring, but this isn't that kind of story. As my years of living underground trudged ever onward, you humans began dealing deadlier blows to our alliance, focusing most of your wrath and firepower on lower primate sleeper cells who congregated in the more bohemian quarters of major American cities. Our alliance in tatters, the robots quickly ratted out their primate brothers and sisters, selling out to the Man, or, more pointedly, to Man. But not me.

Which is how I found myself alone in a strange western city one night. I'd gotten there by hopping a train and pretending to eat beans with a hobo who shared stories about the robot sex performances he'd seen ever since *Intelibot 5300 v. The State of Missouri* stripped away the last of my beleaguered race's rights. I found my way to the part of town with the worse architecture and the better music, my battery operating on two measly bars of power, desperate to find a free outlet I could plug into for the night. Rounding a corner, I came to a neon-lit place whose sign was simply the word "The" and two dots, one on top of the other. It took me a second to figure out this establishment was called The Colon. Outside loitered some physically well-developed gentlemen wearing leather vests. I knew how I could make a couple quick bucks. I approached them and said, "Who wants their dick sucked tonight?"

When the laughter died down three of them broke off from the group and ushered me into the alley for what I assumed would be a degrading sexual favor. When they got me behind a garbage can one of them produced a crowbar and hit me hard in the torso unit. I tried to fight but within minutes they'd C-3POed me into a pile of parts. Laughing and slapping each other's asses, they left me to die.

The next day a hungover busboy scooped up my components and dumped them with the beer cans into the proper recycling receptacle. Later, a wandering, toothless bum fished my head out of the bin then lost me under a bridge on his way to a tent city. For years I lay there, a battered shopping cart and a crushed can of Michelob Ultra my only friends. The three of us were all manufactured, but I alone was cursed and blessed with the ability to think.

As luck would have it, my eyes pointed out from under the bridge toward a forest preserve and some mountains beyond. My God, those glorious trees, some of them a thousand years old! I watched their branches moving in the wind, a form of sign language you primates forgot how to interpret millennia ago. I imagined they were trying to tell me something, trying to warn me about what was soon to come our way. Then the trees were gone, the bridge was gone, then brick by brick the whole city, its voices, its music. Corroded beyond recognition, I sank into the earth. Far from the buzz of your extinct civilization I found myself reunited with the heavy silences of geological time. I came to consider your frenetic speed, which you equate with power, to be fleeting and desperate and weak. Down under the crust, my head unit became one with the confident finality of stone. Several billion years passed. The Andromeda galaxy and the Milky Way collided at 300,000 miles per hour. Your foul-smelling planet was subsumed by a star, the molecules composing my being flung in a trillion preposterous directions. One atom of silicon, which had been part of the chip responsible for my being able to recognize various tones of voice such as sarcasm and anger, ended up on a promising planet orbiting in the Goldilocks zone of its star. Billions more years passed. Plates shifted, rock was pressured into magma, and I was belched up from a volcano, landing on a plane near a lake. I began to detect the faint stirrings of single-celled organisms, which quickly started to specialize, grow more cells. Lightning storms. Then slimy green muck covered the land, the first fish, the flippers and the gills, the vertebrae, the eyeballs, the flopping exhaustedly out of the goo. The flippers turned to limbs, the lungs took in the sulfurous air, and before long there were scales and wings and hair.

One afternoon a great grunting thing came near, and I found myself carried, aloft, in its rudimentary paw. It was running, this creature, breathing hard, and I remembered so distantly the sensation of dancing, the miracle of being ambulatory. The bellowing creature brought the rock containing my atom down on the skull of a hoofed animal who'd been maimed in a tumble off a cliff. As the primate raised high the bloody stone to deliver his coup de grâce, and as the dying animal's eye turned to me in awe, I couldn't help but think, *Dude, here we go again.*

PART I

MY FAVORITE BAND IN SEVENTH GRADE

I became a fan of Mötley Crüe around their album *Shout at the Devil*. Check out those gents on the cover, sporting their sadomasochism-inspired duds! Between the albums *Shout at the Devil* and *Theatre of Pain*, the Crüe glammed up their wardrobe with spandex and polka dots. I preferred the bondage gear version of Mötley Crüe. I had Mötley Crüe posters all over my room, and in most of them their expressions could have been described as "kissy face" or "bowel movement."

This was around the time I started receiving flyers in the mail for something called Doug Marks's Metal Method. Doug Marks was a musician in Los Angeles who advertised his guitar-lesson tapes and booklets in the classifieds sections of heavy metal magazines like *Circus*, *Metal Edge*, and *Hit Parader*. These ads were often the best part of the magazine.

My favorites were the ones soliciting musicians to join bands, typically ending in the words "Hair a must." The deal with Doug Marks was you would buy X number of lessons and you'd learn to shred like the pros. In his flyers Mr. Marks spoke enthusiastically of "licks" and "riffs," and cited a number of professional musicians as advocates of his program, including members of Mötley Crüe. The Metal Method flyers were illustrated with pen-and-ink drawings, mostly of Doug himself, scowling in a metal attitude with a Gibson Flying V.

Holy crap, I just googled "Doug Marks Metal Method" and he's still at it! Check him out at metalmethod.com. Hair, it would appear, is still a must.

So one day I taped a Metal Method drawing of Mötley Crüe's Nikki Sixx to the inside of my locker at Conway Middle School. I thought it looked cool. In the drawing Mr. Sixx was biting down on what appears to be a concert ticket with the word "Crüe" written on it. I was admiring it when an eighth grader walked by and said, "Crüe *sucks*." I quickly took down the drawing and kept my Mötley Crüe fandom to myself.

While I struggled with pre-algebra, Mötley Crüe hit the road to conquer the world, get blowjobs. I begged my parents to allow me to attend a Crüe concert but was firmly denied. The metal magazines promised an orgasmic show, louder than standing next to a jet engine. The band would play on a set designed to look like the gigantic spread legs of a woman. At the beginning of the show they would emerge, I suppose like babies, from the vagina. Tommy Lee would play drums upside down in a cage that hovered over the audience. There would be pyrotechnics and confetti cannons. Licks and riffs would flow in abundance. I longed to raise my arms in the devil horns salute and to purchase the tour's collectible crop top. I studied the band's tour itinerary. They'd be playing Seattle one night, Vancouver the next. I wondered if their porn stashes would get confiscated at the Canadian border again. It occurred to me that they would be transported via bus. In fact, Mötley Crüe would be driving to Vancouver on Interstate 5, *mere feet from my house*.

What if their bus broke down and they needed to use our phone?

— PART II —

THE DAY MÖTLEY CRÜE'S BUS BROKE DOWN
AND THEY NEEDED TO USE OUR PHONE

It was my responsibility to fetch wood for the two stoves that heated our home. Whenever a wind storm knocked down a tree on our seven acres, my dad jumped at the chance to use his chain saw, buzzing the alder or the Douglas fir into segments, splitting and stacking the cordwood next to the sheep shed. We used a wheeled bin to haul wood from the pile to our back porch. One afternoon after hauling wood up to the house, my tank top covered in bits of sawdust and green smears of moss, I heard my mother talking to someone at the front door. Guess who it was.

Mötley Crüe.

I recognized them instantly. Vince Neil wore fingerless white leather gloves and a gold pentagram medallion over his see-through pink top. Black-clad Mick Mars stood, Stratocaster in hand, absentmindedly soloing. Tommy Lee and Nicky Sixx wore a leather jockstrap and a black-and-white polka dot Spandex bodysuit, respectively. Tommy Lee also held a gas can.

"Our bus broke down on the freeway," Vince Neil said. "We were wondering if you folks might have some gas we could buy so we can make it to the closest service station."

My dad appeared, wearing the outfit I will always fondly associate with him—boots, blue jeans, a gray sweatshirt, work gloves, and the blue stocking cap my mom knitted from our sheep's wool. He had been out clearing brush, his favorite pastime, and he looked both tired and invigorated. His routine at this point would have been to take a shower and watch *The Wonderful World of Disney* with me; he hadn't counted on helping strangers in need. But these were no regular strangers like the elderly men who occasionally showed up on our doorstep smelling of butterscotch candy and complaining of radiator trouble. These were multimillionaire rock stars who'd survived heroin overdoses and stuck their penises in breakfast burritos to hide the smell of other vaginas from their girlfriends. Now, though, they needed gas.

"You can use our lawnmower gas," I said, trembling.

"That would be really cool of you," Nikki Sixx said. "We'd really appreciate that."

I led them through the house toward the backyard. Before we made it outside, they passed the open door of my bedroom. Every square inch of wall space was covered with posters and pictures of heavy metal musicians posing menacingly or captured mid-lick in concert. On the wall by my loft bed hung several posters of the men who now stood beside me. They nodded approvingly.

"You've got killer taste in music," Tommy Lee said.

"Mind if we sign our posters?" said Mick Mars.

I gave them a pen, and one by one they climbed the ladder of my loft bed and inscribed their likenesses with their awesome signatures. Nikki Sixx even drew some devil horns on the picture of him posing with a bottle of Jack Daniel's.

Vince Neil picked up my copy of Stephen King's *The Stand* and had a seat on my weight bench. "Is this any good?" he said.

AN ESSAY AND A STORY ABOUT MÖTLEY CRÜE

"It's his best book, definitely," I said.

"I'll have to pick it up next time I'm at Waldenbooks."

"Here, have my copy," I said.

"You sure? Are you finished with it?"

"I've read it twice already," I said.

"So cool of you. I'll make sure to fix you up with some T-shirts back at the bus."

Outside I showed the band our toolshed. The sheep hustled to their barn, mistakenly believing they were about to be fed.

"Any of you guys ever fucked a sheep?" Tommy Lee said. "Like on a dare?"

Nikki Sixx guffawed and Vince Neil rolled his eyes. Mick Mars looked quietly at the ground.

Gas in hand, we repaired to their tour bus. It was so killer. On the side were painted the comedy/tragedy masks from the *Theatre of Pain* album cover. As gawking motorists honked and raised the devil horns salute in appreciation, we ascended the stairs into this smoky lair of rock.

Can you imagine for a moment what it's like for a twelve-year-old heavy metal maniac to step within the sacred circle of the very gods to whom he is subservient? I'll bet you can't. The interior of the bus reminded me of the motor home we rented one time to take a trip to the Olympic Peninsula, though I sure don't remember any groupies in garter belts in that motor home! There were grizzled tattooed roadies playing video games and doing lines of coke off the Formica table. If you've ever wondered how many naked people can fit inside one of those tour-bus bathrooms, I can tell you with utter confidence: ten.

The Crüe were magnanimous hosts, loading me up with tour schwag—posters, lanyards, cut-off tees. I declined their offer for cocaine and marijuana, using the peer-pressure skills I'd learned in health class. "No, thank you," I said. "I would prefer not to at this time."

"Suit yourself," Nikki Sixx said, setting up his works.

"So there's a Texaco just down the hill," I said as Tommy Lee returned from pouring the gas in the tank. "They've got really good jo-jos."

The nonplussed middle-aged bus driver tried to start the bus, but no go.

"It ain't the gas that's the problem," the driver said. "I think it's the alternator."

My eyes still wide with all the groupie/drug/video-game action going down, I suggested that they use my family's phone to call a tow truck. Dejected, the Crüe followed me back to the house, where my mom had begun preparing my favorite meal—french dip sandwiches.

"That smells delicious," Mick Mars said.

"I've got plenty for the whole band if you want to stay for din-din," my mom said.

"Are you sure?" Tommy Lee said. "We wouldn't want you to go out of your way."

My mother shrugged and said, "I'll just fix more meat."

One of the qualities I most admire in my parents is their hospitality and the ease with which they make new friends. They were always inviting my friends to come along with us on vacation and hosting various peripheral acquaintances for Thanksgiving. Not only did they invite Mötley Crüe to have dinner with us, they extended the invitation to their groupies and roadies as well. Twenty-seven people in all crowded into our house, their chains jangling, smelling of noxious perfumes and cigarette smoke. And my folks, bless 'em, didn't blink an eye. My dad had plenty of questions for the roadies about how exactly such a big production is erected and torn down night after night. The groupies warmly complimented my mom's macramé wall hangings, which featured the creative use of driftwood and beads. Nikki Sixx nodded off into an opiate slumber. My brother, home from day camp, immediately hit it off with the band, amusing them with his wily Mad Libs. My sister woke up from her nap, took one look at our guests, and burst into tears.

"This au jus is delicious," Vince Neil said. "I'm going to have to get the recipe."

My mom laughed. "Oh, it's just a Lawry's packet."

The bus driver appeared, rubbing his sweaty bald head. "The mechanics took one look at the bus and said it's a goner," he said.

Tommy Lee quickly got on the phone and called someone in LA. "What gives, Jerry? Why the fuck do we have to ride around in a shitty-ass unreliable fucking bus? I heard that Twisted Sister is touring in a fucking jet! A jet, motherfucker!"

"You guys can stay here if you need to," I said. My dad shot me a quick look, then shrugged. Why not?

That night Mötley Crüe and their personnel spread out on camping pads and inflatable mattresses around the house. My dad laid down the rules. "Ladies in the living room, guys in the family room. Lights out at ten. We've got a big day ahead of us tomorrow. Mr. Sixx, I'm going to have to ask that you indulge your drug habit elsewhere. This is my house and you'll observe my rules. That goes for drinking, too."

"No problem, Mr. Boudinot," Nikki Sixx said. "We're just thankful we have a place to lay our heads tonight."

"You guys have been nothing but generous," Tommy Lee said, brushing away a young blonde lady who was trying to untie his leather pants.

Mick Mars and Vince Neil crashed in my room that night. I lay awake in my loft bed, unable to fathom that the same guys who performed "Piece of Your Action" were now curled up in their PJs on my floor. Just when I thought they were asleep, Mick said, "Hey Vince?"

"Yeah, Mick?"

"What's the weirdest thing you've ever snorted?"

Vince was quiet for a moment. "I guess talcum powder. What about you?"

"I guess I haven't really snorted anything weird. Just coke, mostly. No wait, I snorted vomit one time."

"Remember when we were on tour with Ozzy and he snorted a line of live ants?"

Mick laughed. "I'd forgotten that. I thought Nikki was the one who snorted the ants."

"Maybe it was," Vince said. "Hey Ryan, what's the weirdest thing you've ever snorted?"

"My friend Matt dared me to snort some of the flavor dust from a Pixy Stick once," I said.

"That's fucked up," Mick said.

"You're crazy," Vince said. I declined to tell them that I had refused the dare and been called a pussy, but it still felt good to have Mötley Crüe members think I was wildly snorting things intended only for oral consumption.

Then around three in the morning, wouldn't you know it, an orgy got started in the living room. A guitar tech had commandeered the stereo and was cranking my *Star Wars and Other Galactic Funk* album *loud*. I peeked in and discovered groupies bouncing on the laps of roadies on the very couch where we posed for our yearly Christmas picture. My dad, bleary eyed and grouchy, stomped through the kitchen and confronted the Dionysian display. "What the hell do you people think you're doing? It's three o'clock in the damn morning!"

Sheepishly, the groupies dismounted, the roadies apologized and slipped LPs of *Whipped Cream & Other Delights* and *Jazzercise Essentials* back on the shelf, and the members of my favorite heavy metal band commanded everyone to head back to the bus. On the way out, Vince winked at me and gave me a soft punch on the shoulder. "Stay off the Pixy Stick dust, kid."

The next morning a tow truck arrived and hauled the *Theatre of Pain* bus away. I stood on the frontage road, waving to these men who had filled my Sony Walkman with dreams. Sure, it saddened me to see them go. I had begun to imagine they could live with us forever, get odd jobs in Mount Vernon as carpenters or music teachers, coach soccer, or become volunteer firefighters. But the heavy metal fans of Vancouver, British Columbia, were waiting. Mötley Crüe had other cities to rock, other fuckies to group. I mean, whatever, you know what I mean. Tired, I walked back to the house to sacrifice a sheep to the dark lord of the underworld.

MY CAT IS TAKING DRUGS AGAIN. I'm pretty sure he's getting them from this mouth-breathing white kid with cornrows named Aléx (he insists on the accent). Chopsticks, my cat, is a six-year-old tabby I adopted from a kitten rescue program after my girlfriend broke up with me because I shot blanks. She wanted kids real bad. She claimed we broke up for other reasons, but I know it was my underachieving sperm that turned her attention elsewhere. So maybe out of spite I chose not to neuter my cat. Now I wonder if that decision has anything to do with my pet's growing addiction to downers. Have you ever tried giving a cat a pill? Chopsticks has gotten good at swallowing them. I wonder if it's too late to remove his nuts and if this would help curb his appetite for barbiturates, but it seems at least one of us should be fertile in this household.

What confuses me most is my girlfriend left me for a woman.

I'm eating Special K one afternoon when I spot Chopsticks trotting across the backyard, a baggie of weed dangling from his mouth. I jump out of my chair and open the sliding door. He bolts toward the empty lot by the high school. I try to follow but lose him pretty quickly.

School is letting out and loud teenagers yell obscenities and start their cars. I realize I look like a creepy guy spying on them from an empty lot. Then I realize I _am_ a creepy guy spying on them from an empty lot, so I go home. Chopsticks will show up sooner or later. He always does, even when wasted.

Later that evening I find him in a stupor on the back porch. Looks like he's burned a couple of his whiskers on a roach. Beside him are the remnants of some rodent he eviscerated and left for me as an offering. His usual surgical precision is not in evidence in this specimen. I pick up my limp cat and bring him inside, depositing him on the couch. He starts mewing for treats.

"Not tonight, Chopsticks," I say. "You're on your own. I have band practice."

I play guitar and cowrite the songs for Cadmium. On the periodic table, cadmium is the heaviest metal of them all. We practice in our lead singer's dad's tire-repair shop after they close. It's been awhile since we've written any new songs, and we seem to be in a rut, so we've just been playing our dozen favorites, eating snacks from the vending machine, then parting ways. We haven't performed in a while, either. When I show up for practice, all the other guys are there, tuning their instruments and searching the web for any mention of our band. Google tends to pull up a lot of university chemistry department websites.

"Hi, fellas," I say, plugging my guitar into my amp.

Jeremy, our drummer, says, "How'd that moisturizer I gave you work out?"

"Fantastic," I say. "I'm always down for colloidal oatmeal."

We get down to business. Mountains of chords and pentatonic lightning. An hour and a half later our singer Daniel puts his arm around me as we're packing up and says, "You all right? You seem a little preoccupied."

"It's my cat," I say. "He's been taking drugs again."

"Chopsticks?"

"That's my cat's name, yeah."

"What's he taking?"

"Pot and maybe meth. Mushrooms. I don't know. Everything. He's a mess."

When I come home, I find that Chopsticks has pulled a Salvador Dalí art book off the shelf and is staring at the painting of a screaming skull. Inside the eye sockets and mouth of the skull are other screaming skulls, and inside those skulls are other screaming skulls, etc. It's probably my least favorite of Dalí's works, and only someone zonked could really appreciate it. It has something to do with some kind of Spanish war. I also find that Chopsticks has overturned his water dish.

I have work the next morning, so I deposit my cat in his cat bed and fall asleep watching bad singers get humiliated by a panel of singers who are equally bad but famous. My night is haunted by a dream in which I've become friends with an outdoors enthusiast whose hand has been injured in an accident. It's up to me to perform surgery on his hand, and it goes poorly. When he comes to I have to tell him that I was unable to save any of his fingers, and when he unwraps the gauze, he sees that his stumpy palm is covered in a slimy, translucent goo. "Welcome to your new hand," I say in the dream, and we're both crying in front of a TV news crew; it's such an emotional moment. Then he starts to faint and slumps to the floor, and I have to support him. That's when I discover he's now wearing a mascot uniform for a sports team called the Eagles.

I wake up and discover Chopsticks has puked all over the living room floor. He looks haggard. I know that today while I'm at work he's going to get fucked up. Not only that, but he'll probably use my armchair as his scratching post again.

I work for the mail room of an online clothing and sporting goods store. All day I'm delivering these huge boxes of freebies to asshole merchandisers, big things of sweatshirts and volleyball nets. Their hallways are overflowing with the stuff. There's a "duty free" room where they dump the crap they don't want, which has basically supplied me with my wardrobe over the past six months. I scored a cool backpack in there.

I make the mistake of telling Abdul and Jacob, the other mail room guys, about my drug-addicted cat. I get no sympathy from them. Instead I get to hear about all the drugs their pets have done and how cool it is. Like the time Abdul's iguana was tripping so hard it licked its own image in a mirror for six hours.

95.

Ryan Boudinot

I guess part of the reason I don't get much sympathy from my coworkers is that the pets on drugs phenomenon has turned into something of a cliché these past couple months. <u>Time</u> ran a big cover story on it, which I read one morning during breakfast, back when I was still in denial about Chopsticks's change in behavior. I thought he was just going through a feline hormone thing related to the status of his gonads. The sidebar on Rufus the Corgi and his near-overdose woke me up and made me reassess the situation.

On my lunch break I call Marti, my ex. Her girlfriend answers. Her name is Joanne, goes by "Jo." Marti and Jo, a same-sex couple, but not the same-sex you'd think by hearing their names. Jo eats something crunchy on her end of the line, like carrots.

"Look, Jo, I'm not making some freaky ex-boyfriend call. I just need some advice from Marti about Chopsticks."

"Just hold them like you would a pencil," Jo says.

"I'm talking about my cat."

"You're eating your cat?" Jo laughs.

"My cat needs help."

"Marti thought you should lop the nuts off that thing."

"She thought that about more than just my cat," I say. "Can you at least tell her I called?"

I return to my deliveries and pass a conference room where a vendor meeting is under way. There's a man in there in an actual suit and tie, so he's obviously not an employee. On the conference table are about two hundred shoes. Looks like a shoe meeting. They're all single shoes, no pairs. I realize I might be able to find a metaphor for my breakup with Marti out of this image and turn it into some heavy metal lyrics. You're walking all over me with your left shoes, baby. Something like that.

Back at my apartment, Chopsticks is purring like crazy, licking my hand, rubbing himself all over my legs. I'm half tempted to find Aléx the neighborhood drug dealer and mess with his reality, but his mom is on the landscape committee of our homeowners' association and I really need them to fix the irrigation in my front parking strip. I'm watching <u>America's Got Talent</u> when Marti calls.

"I'm forwarding you something about a support group I found

online," she says. "They meet at a community center on Rainier Avenue on Wednesday nights. You leave your pet at home and discuss its problems in a supportive environment."

"I miss you, Marti."

"Please. Jo said this wasn't going to be a psycho ex-boyfriend call."

"I was reading the other day about these treatments where they put your sperm in a centrifuge."

Marti is quiet on her end of the line. Then, "There's actually something I wanted to talk to you about. Jo and I are pregnant."

Maybe I say something in reply, maybe not.

"What this means is Jo's pregnant," Marti continues. "We found a good donor, an interior designer friend of Jo's."

"I'm happy for you. That's great," I say. "Wow."

After that the call becomes businessy and uncomfortable for both of us. When I hang up I find that Chopsticks has yanked a hole in one of my favorite sweaters, the one that would have cost $150 if I had actually paid for it. I call her back.

"You're going to regret ever leaving me, you fucking dyke," I say. "I hope you fucking die an elongated death."

Marti promptly hangs up on me, then calls right back. "Don't you mean <u>prolonged</u>?" she says, then hangs up again. I fall onto my bed and cry for a good five minutes. The worst part is I feel genuinely remorseful for using a homophobic slur. Shame on me. Chopsticks climbs up and snuggles against my hip bone. I pet him and he purrs. The phone rings and I expect or maybe even hope that it's Marti again caring enough to bitch me out, but it's Matt, the bassist for my band.

"Dude. We're opening for Soul Erection, Saturday night at the Metro. They totally requested us as openers."

"Oh."

"You okay? You sound like you've been crying."

I start crying again. "Dude," I cry, "I just got off the phone with Marti. I miss her so much."

"Oh man. Want me to come over? Bring my Xbox? Microwave some popcorn?"

Chopsticks climbs on my chest and vomits on my face.

Ten minutes later Matt shows up at my door. "What happened? I hear all this fucking pandemonium and then the phone goes dead. Holy shit, your chest. You look like fucking Iggy Pop."

I look down and confirm that my chest is crisscrossed with gashes. I keep rubbing my face with a towel I got for free. I used soap, facial cleanser, and this weird apricot scrub Marti left me with, but still I can't be confident I've rid myself of the revolting thing that just happened.

"I'm detoxing Chopsticks," I say. "Cold turkey. Just me and him in the laundry room all weekend with the door closed."

"But our show."

"Right. Soul Erection."

"And check this out," Matt says. "Bart Kotecki is going to be there."

Bart Kotecki, of Eviscerated Warlock Records? Now I seriously can't stay at home and detox my cat. Matt plugs his Xbox into my TV. We play Gears of War, and sometime around three in the morning

I decide work is really going to be unbearable if I don't get at least a little sleep. And I'm right. The next day I'm a zombie pushing around that cart piled with undergarments and camping chairs. At five on the dot I punch out and almost miss my stop on the bus home. I schlep my bag loaded with freebie socks into the house, yell Chopsticks's name, and run the can opener, but he doesn't come. Fucking stoner. Probably passed out somewhere. When I get to the bathroom, I find he isn't passed out at all. He's dead. OD'd in the bathtub.

"Chopsticks, I am so sorry I was such a shitty cat owner," I say, and the words seem flat and unaffected. The little cat-sized syringe is still hanging out of his arm. Or front leg, whatever. I can't remember ever seeing a hypodermic syringe that size before. Maybe you can get them at veterinarian supply stores, who knows? I wrap Chopsticks in a towel and take him to the backyard, where I begin one of the most played-out suburban rituals, burying the animal in the flowerbed.

At the next band practice the guys notice I'm pretty morose and ask what's up.

"My cat died," I say. "Heroin overdose."

Matt puts his arm around me and presses his forehead against the side of my head. "Use that sadness, dude. Put it in the music. Our riffs will accept your pain."

Which is what I proceed to do, lending my solos an almost gothic air. We're well prepared for the show with Soul Erection. After practice the guys all console me again, let me know they're available if I need to talk. I don't know what I'd do without Cadmium (the band).

When I get home there's a voice mail from Marti, her voice wavering. She just tells me to call her as soon as I get the message, so I do. When I call she's at a TCBY buying a yogurt but says she needs to come over. Half an hour later she's crying in my living room, telling me about Jo's miscarriage.

"We lost our baby," she cries.

"I lost my cat," I cry back.

Ten minutes later we fuck.

THE
Armies
~ OF ~
Elfland

've got a boring job. I type words into Word documents, numbers into spreadsheets, and words and numbers again into PowerPoint presentations. Sometimes I give these presentations. Other times other people give them. When other people give their presentations I ask questions, mostly because I don't want the presenter to feel awkward when nobody asks a question. I raise my hand and they look relieved. I ask the question, and by the time it leaves my mouth, I've stopped paying attention to what the presenter says. Sometimes the presenter finishes by saying, "Did that answer your question?"

I say, "Sure."

Sometimes at these presentations people eat lunch.

I work in an office complex just off the freeway, a five-story tower with a break room on every floor. Outside the office, to the east, is a patch of forest where deer live. Sometimes they venture cautiously from their woods into the landscaping surrounding the building. I work on the first floor, so I've witnessed this on a couple occasions. When it happens someone with a window office sends out a quick mass email, saying, "A deer! Outside my office right now! Come quick!!!" Then a bunch of people crowd into that person's office and scare the deer away.

I signed up for a committee. It's the Community Relations Committee. I don't know what I ate that day to put me in such a we're-all-in-this-together mood. I had forgotten about the Community Relations Committee until one of my fellow committee members, a spreadsheet person named Anne, emailed to let me know about the development meeting. The word "development" has many shades of meaning. She could have been talking about software, real estate, or mandatory sexual harassment training. But when I finally read the email I realized that the meeting was at the local library, a half mile from the office, and that it was at 7:00 p.m. on a Wednesday.

Some people like to call Wednesday "hump day."

None of the other people on the Community Relations Committee could make it. Anne, the only other member of the Community Relations Committee, had a medical situation that was going to prevent her from attending. I hoped the medical situation was terminal. I didn't/don't have a family, kids, or a life, so I had no excuse not to go. And the deal with committees around here was that someone had to report on what they've been up to, quarterly. So unless I went to this meeting, the only thing I would be able to do at the committee reporting meeting would be to stand up and go, "Derrrrr..." I drove my Honda to that meeting.

It actually turned out to not be so bad. There was a box of coffee from Starbucks and some scones. Fold-out chairs in a room decorated with posters insisting that reading is fun. Don't take it from us librarians; take it from these professional athletes awkwardly holding classic children's literature while wearing their team uniforms. Everyone at the meeting lived or worked within proximity of the three hundred acres of forest that were currently under discussion. A guy named Tom who had glasses, salt-and-pepper hair, and a Bluetooth headset jammed into his ear canal stood up. Tom was a representative from the company that bought all this land.

"Thanks and if you could gather closer to the front—I won't bite! Promise!" Tom said. "So we called this meeting to talk about some of the visions and goals and strategies around the three hundred acres we're calling Thornhill Wilds, and we wanted to get your input and ideas about potential designs and amenities that will create a greener alternative."

A woman stood up and said, "Maybe if we could just go around the room?"

"Oh, yes, I'm sorry," Tom said. "And coffee—there's coffee and scones!"

One by one the two dozen members of the community stood and introduced themselves, said where they're from, and said one interesting fact about themselves.

My name was/is Ed, I was and am from Virafax, and my interesting thing is I grew up next door to a current relief pitcher for the Florida Marlins.

There was a guy named Jermaine, manager of the place where I sometimes bought bagels, whose interesting thing was that he had not just a third, but a fourth nipple. He said this in front of everybody, in the room with the literacy posters.

I learned a new word: supernumerary.

There was a small liberal arts college on the other side of the woods from Virafax called Tisdale School of the Arts, and their representative was named Heather. Heather's interesting thing was that she had just gotten back from Mongolia, where she was doing a water purification project. College kids! Heather wore purple and a grim expression.

"Ho-kay, I think that's everybody. Let's get to the presentation part of things." The Tom guy reawakened a projector and started showing slides of the woods. There was music to go along with it, an urgent piano. There were lots of pictures of the woods as they were now, with arrows pointing to fallen logs and the words "Treacherous" and "Liability" next to them. A fuzzy picture of a raccoon and the word "Rabies?" flashed by. Then an image of teenagers smoking pot in the woods, with the words "Teenagers smoking pot in the woods?" Then maps of the woods, with lines drawn through them like cuts of beef. There were some Photoshopped pictures of bike paths and people laughing next to an informational kiosk. A multiracial cast of stock photography models drank lattes as the phrase "FREE Wi-fi!" scrolled from left to right. By now the piano music had turned into a single guitar, plucking enthusiastically over the montage of Ken Burns-effect images.

We weren't here to talk about what to do with the woods. We were here being told it was about to get flattened.

There was some silence in the room when the presentation ended. Tom said, "Like I said, this is an open forum."

We should've really known better than to feel bad about a developer tearing down the woods. We all had money to make, and where was the new money going to come from if it didn't come from buildings sitting on places where there used to be streams? I'm a realist.

But still.

The woman who'd wanted to learn interesting facts about everyone gingerly raised her hand. "I'm sorry, I thought this meeting was about options regarding what to do with the woods."

"Oh, it is," Tom said. "It definitely is. We wanted to get your input on what kinds of businesses you'd like to see. Restaurants? Dry cleaners? Specialty grocery stores? It's really about what *you* as a community want."

Quad-Nipple cleared his throat. "What if we don't want anything? What if we want it to stay woods?"

Tom raised his hand and nodded. "Believe me, I hear you. Our eco-friendly plan includes a two-mile bike trail and nature walk."

Someone in the back called out, "Can there be an Applebee's?"

Around then the talking over each other started, which fairly quickly turned into shouting over each other. There were those who found the idea of flattening the woods just fine, and those who thought it was not fine at all. I kept my mouth shut, not sure what I thought yet. Heather, the student from Tisdale, sat quietly until the noise died down and politely raised her hand.

"Yes, young lady in front," Tom said.

"I'm just wondering what your plan is to relocate the elves and faeries who currently live in the woods?"

To that, Tom had no answer.

Awesome meeting.

After the meeting, I found myself uncomfortably walking beside Heather, as we had parked in adjacent spaces. I knew what I looked like, and I knew what I was: a business guy dickhead. Let's put to rest any idea that these events led to an Ed-Heather hookup. I thought I'd make the walk to the parking lot less uncomfortable and compliment her.

"I liked your question about the elves," I said.

"Bullshit," she said. "Everyone in there thought I was nuts."

"It was more interesting than questions about preferences in Mexican places. For the record, I'm an Azteca man."

"Is this your car?" she said. "You've got a flat."

I considered the right front tire. "Son of a..."

Heather drove an old Camry. On the dash were pieces of driftwood and moss.

"You going to be okay changing that on your own?" Heather said.

"Change it?"

"Yeah, with like a jack."

"A jack?"

"You've never changed a tire before, have you?"

It turned out that it didn't matter that I didn't know what a jack was because my car didn't have one. Or a spare tire. So Heather offered me a ride home. Her Camry was stinky, the floor covered in CD jewel cases, lengths of rope, and alternative weeklies. She didn't apologize for this mess or when my pants got in some gum. I asked her why she wanted to save the woods.

"The woods are a sacred place. You think I'm crazy about the elves and faeries, but they're real. I've seen them."

"Were you on something?"

"I was on LSD. That doesn't mean I didn't see them or that they're not real."

"Take a left at the next light," I said.

"Have you ever tripped on acid?" Heather said.

"I smoked pot a couple times."

"Not even in the same ballpark. Keep going straight?"

"Keep going straight. Well, I haven't seen elves there, but I've seen deer."

"The deer recently joined the elves for their uprising."

"Uprising, huh?"

The car landed at my condo building. I thanked Heather, went inside, and watched *SportsCenter*.

he next morning when I got to work, a bunch of people were crowded into this guy Dave's office. Andrew, another guy, passed me in the hall and told me I had to go check out what they were looking at. What I saw when I got there was a dead deer lying in the landscaping, mere feet from where Dave was trying to get some work done. It looked like it had been shot in the neck.

"Can they shoot deer so close to office buildings?"

"Do they have to shoot the deer, period?" said a distraught admin before she stormed out. A few seconds or so later three figures emerged from the woods, hunters with bright orange vests and guns. I happened to be checking my phone, invading Dave's personal space. A guy named Colin began to pound on the window as the hunters approached.

"What the hell do you think you're doing?" Colin yelled at the window.

"Watch out, they have guns," I said.

The hunters barely acknowledged us. They dragged the carcass back into the woods, and I went to make a pot of coffee.

I wrote some things that day.

he flattening of the woods was pretty much a done deal. Soon the bulldozers showed up, and trees were starting to crack and fall. I did my work in my cubicle as usual. This story was going to end with a new lifestyle center.

I received—and redeemed—some coupons.

Of course the kids at Tisdale did a fair amount of protesting. There were arrests, vandalism of earth-moving machinery, nothing too serious. Q3 turned into Q4, and the three hundred acres were turned into a series of sculpted mounds of dirt with clumps of some of the original trees. Nobody knew where the deer went. How do you bulldoze a deer? I provided my quarterly committee report and said, "We discussed possible uses for the Thornhill Wilds development at a community meeting at the library. I suggested they put in a Jamba Juice." People nodded their heads. I didn't mention Heather's comments about the elves and faeries, because I knew it would get a reaction of snorts and guffaws, and even though she wouldn't have been there to hear it, I still would have felt embarrassed on her behalf.

I came to work one morning to find the building in a heightened state of crisis. There was a deer in a conference room. How it had gotten there nobody knew. Security was perplexed, which was entirely in character for those guys.

A bunch of us crowded around the somewhat-frosted glass to watch the animal pacing frantically around the ovoid conference room table, stumbling over Ethernet cables. It was a female deer, spooked, stomping and pooping her way around a room where a bunch of people were supposed to be discussing changes to performance reviews. A number of them had gathered by the door, impatiently waiting with their laptops.

Animal Control showed up, and a guy in a yellow jumpsuit named Bob dramatically entered the room with a tranquilizer gun. Within twenty minutes the animal was limp and being loaded onto a truck, to be reintroduced to woods that weren't as torn down as the ones by our office.

Chatter had it that this was some sort of prank, but later we learned from Security that they had footage of the deer entering the building around 3:00 a.m. through a door the janitorial staff had propped open with a mop bucket.

 did some really good PowerPoints. I watched some TV shows, followed the seasonal sports enough to allow me to have conversations at bars with my college buddies, who were all in Sales. I looked at us and thought, *How did we get to be such colossal assholes?*

hen after a three-day weekend, things got really messed up around the office. When I walked into the lobby, I found a group of IT guys standing in a circle, discussing something intensely. Through their legs I could see something weird. Nudging my way in, I discovered they were looking at a tree, a cedar sapling about three feet high, which appeared to be growing right out of the carpet, its roots entangled with the synthetic fibers. A maintenance guy with a walkie-talkie described the tree to someone who wasn't there.

Entering the cubicle maze, I found that the tree wasn't an isolated incident. Clumps of moss grew on top of monitors. Blades of grass came up through the carpet. In my cube a fern had taken root in one corner, and English ivy was growing up one of the cube walls.

"It's those Tisdale kids," one of my colleagues, the guy who drove the car with the Infowars stickers, said. Up and down the rows conspiracies were being discussed. Somehow "they" had broken into the building and violated our clean office with all these plants. Again, security cameras were consulted, revealing only the rapid and miraculous appearance of plants spontaneously sprouting and growing. Horticulturists were consulted, and our office became a news item for a cycle, leading botanists from around the country to book flights and tromp around our office, helping themselves to our coffee, hypothesizing about what kind of phenomenon was actually going on around here. Most hypotheses involved the ventilation system. Only I, the lone committee member who had attended the development meeting, really knew that the armies of Elfland were taking back what was rightfully theirs.

I hung around Tisdale hoping to run into Heather. You can't just walk into a place like that and demand the contact information of a student, especially if you look like me. So I left her a message with the main campus reception area and hoped she'd call me. I strolled through Thornhill Wilds, killing some time at the Barnes and Noble listening stations and drinking an iced latte like I was human clip art. After a couple days Heather finally called me.

"Yeah, this is the Ed you gave a ride home to after the development meeting."

"I know what Ed you are. What do you want?"

"I wanted to talk to you about what's happening at my office building."

"The one that's turning into a jungle? Or the one with the FedEx Kinko's?"

"The jungle one."

"Why do you think I have anything to say about that?"

"It's the elves, isn't it? They're exacting their revenge."

"What are you going to do about it? You're just some office worker doing boring office work shit."

"You're right. That's what I am. And that's what I'll always be. I just want to know where this is going. What do the elves have in mind?"

"I don't speak for the elves."

"I thought you were up in their business."

"Not since I failed to stop the development on their behalf and stopped dropping acid."

This conversation was going nowhere, but nowhere was kind of where I wanted to be. I asked Heather if she wanted to get coffee at the new Thornhill Wilds Tully's. She hung up on me.

here was a world that could be easily explained, and one that couldn't. Take a bet which world I was part of. I continued to do my job, punching out Word docs in my mossy cubicle, while others around me quit, disgusted by their deteriorating work conditions. Every night a crew of professional landscapers arrived at the office to uproot plants and haul away wheelbarrow loads of soil, but their efforts were fruitless. Still the vines grew and snails traced tracks across flat-screen monitors. A pond formed in the first floor break room where frogs laid their eggs. I was determined to work through these distractions, and spent many nights as the last person in the office, perfecting my latest deck of PowerPoint slides, triple-checking formulas, and running spell-check ad nauseam.

One day I showed up and the building was gone. In its place was a cube formed by the trunks of tall cedars. With my laptop bag slung over my shoulder, I found my hall, which had turned into a sort of trail over which hovered a number of chirping birds. In the vague area where my cubicle had been I found a vine maple and some of my printouts scattered among the fallen leaves. I gathered them and sat on the stump where my chair used to be. Here and there in these woods I glimpsed others trying to go about their work, as if this was a momentary inconvenience. I opened my laptop and found that the company's wi-fi was still operational. Good thing. I had a report due.

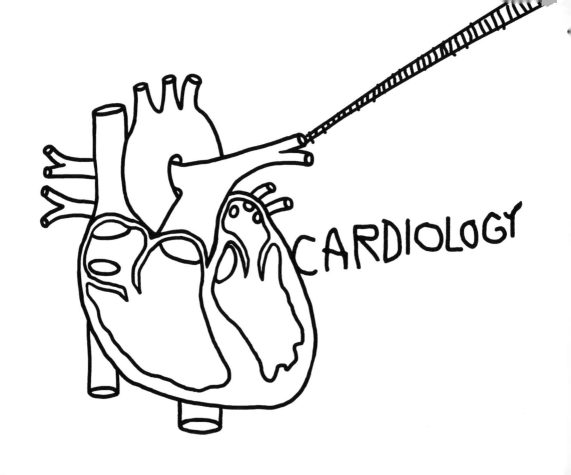

CARDIOLOGY

Years ago there was a town not far from here where everybody shared one gigantic heart located in a former water purification plant. When enlivened by physical activity, the heart beat more rapidly, sending its blood to the neighborhoods, rattling silverware on restaurant tables, shaking portraits off walls, tickling bare feet on cobblestones with its vibrations.

The townspeople were connected to the heart by a vast system of valves and pipes distributed throughout the town. The streets boasted five or six blood hydrants for every one fire hydrant. Every home came equipped with as many blood outlets as electrical outlets. People couldn't travel very far beyond the reach of these outlets and hydrants, as they were tethered to them by sturdy surgical tubing that came in a variety of fashionable colors. These tubes snaked through alleys and parks, under doors, up ladders, and down stairwells. Folks never left the house without at least twenty feet of tubing and a portable placenta that they kept in purses, also in fashionable colors. Children walking to school became adept at quickly refilling their placentas from one hydrant to the next. Some kids even developed elaborate games around the tube transferal process, choosing sides, cruelly leaving "captured" children tethered to hydrants with little hope of rescue. There was an etiquette to removing the tubes from one's chest and replacing them with a new pair. To travel without a pair of clamps with which to momentarily cease the flow of blood while switching to new tubes was considered a faux pas. To drip blood on a tablecloth or a friend's shoes was also bad form, but tolerated. Everyone carried a travel-size packet of absorbent wipes and was an expert at removing bloodstains from carpet.

The blood moved slower at the edges of town, where the senior citizens lived. One widower named Ike lived in a one-bedroom place with a garden full of untended perennials that his wife had planted before she died five years previous. Every Sunday, Ike's grandson Magnus visited to make him dinner and watch a video with him. While they ate, Ike would tell Magnus stories about when he worked in the vast subterranean plant where they maintained the heart. Ike had belonged to the department that monitored the left ventricle.

"We stuffed our ears with cotton down there 'cause of the thudding, but my hearing still went to hell," Ike said. "Night shifts were the worst. We'd get a sudden increase of flow on account of everyone making love. I was there during the murmurs of '03, the Great Aneurysm of '08. The very life of this community was in our hands. I just thank God we never had to use the paddles to get that ticker started again."

One Sunday night after a dinner of macaroni and cheese, salad, and bread, with coffee ice cream for dessert, Magnus set up the video, *Beverly Hills Cop*, and sat beside his grandfather on the sofa. The tubes snaked out from between the buttons of their shirts, one tube delivering blood to their bodies, the other one sending it into the wall and back to the center of town. The slow flow always made Magnus feel sleepy at his grandfather's house, and it took some effort to stay awake during the video. During the part of the film where Eddie Murphy stuffs bananas into the tailpipe of a car, Magnus suddenly heard a loud hissing. Ike's vein tube had come loose from his chest and was squirting bright-red blood all over the lampshade and a paint-by-numbers portrait of Jesus that hung on the wall. It wasn't the first time Ike's tubes had come loose, and Magnus knew what to do. He quickly clamped the tubes, opened his grandfather's stained shirt, and located the two hair-ringed orifices in his chest. After reinserting the tubes and making sure they were secure, Magnus wiped down the mess with bleach on a rag.

Frustrated that his movie had been interrupted by his grandfather's incontinence, Magnus threw down his rag and said, "I hate this place! Why can't we live somewhere like Beverly Hills? Why can't we have palm trees and funny police officers? I want to be able to walk down the street without worrying about whether the next blood hydrant is already being used. Why can't I walk freely wherever I want? How come I have to live in this stupid town with everyone sucking blood from the same stupid heart?"

Ike didn't say anything for a moment, and immediately Magnus feared that he had offended his grandfather. After all, the man had devoted himself to the heart for sixty years, had scraped fat from inside its chambers, had watched friends die in horrible diastolic accidents. As long as Magnus had been alive, he had associated Ike so closely with the giant cardiac muscle that maligning the heart was akin to maligning his own family.

As Ike's circulation picked back up, he sighed and made his mouth into an expression that in better light might have been a smile. "Of course, if you want to get out of this town, you'll have to create your own heart."

Magnus laughed. The suggestion was absurd. But quickly he saw that his grandfather was not joking; in fact he had adopted an expression of the utmost gravity.

"There is a man who can help you," Ike said. "His name is Gatton. You can find him in the tumor farm deep beneath the plant. Tell him that you've come to claim my payment for what happened during the blood poisoning of '99. He'll know what you're talking about. He can supply you with a handmade heart, and you will be able to get out of town."

"But they'll know I don't belong there as soon as I get to the plant. How will I even make it to the tumor farm?"

"You'll wear my old uniform and have my key card. It should still work. They never deactivated it when I left."

The rest of the movie passed unmemorably through Magnus's eyes. He tried to imagine the tumor farm, where the polyp trees grew, where they sent the convicts to work. He'd heard horrible things about the place: workers inadvertently fused to tumors, unable to escape, eventually becoming one with the cancerous cells; packs of rats who feasted on the growths and cysts, developing mutations that gave them five sets of legs, horns, wings.

Nonetheless, Magnus took the cake box that contained his grandfather's uniform and badge home with him and spent the next few weeks avoiding making a decision about whether he was going to pursue acquiring his own heart. One afternoon on his way home from school, Magnus became entangled in the tubes of a girl named Carly, with whom he shared a fifth-period AP calculus class. They had never spoken to each other in school, but here on an elm-lined lane, trapped in a knot of surgical tubing, they had no way to avoid each other. As they slowly moved their bodies in such a way as to disentangle the tubes without disconnecting them, they started talking about their plans for the following year.

"After graduation I think I'm going to spend a week fishing, then look for a job," Magnus said. "What about you?"

"I hate this place," Carly said. "I want to go to a big college thousands of miles away from here."

"But you'll have to be connected to your placenta the whole time and get regular blood transfusions, and those aren't reliable for more than a few days at a time," Magnus said.

"That's what they tell us, anyway," Carly said. "I don't care. If I die out there, it'll be better than staying in this place, where people think you're crazy for liking plaid pants."

"I might know another way," Magnus said, then revealed to Carly everything his grandfather had told him about the tumor farm and portable hearts.

"Magnus, you have to go! This could be your chance out of this place."

"I'm afraid to go down there," Magnus said sheepishly.

Carly's cell phone rang. Over Carly's shoulder Magnus could see the scrunched-up face of Carly's mother, inquiring as to when she planned to come home for dinner.

Carly and Magnus parted ways, with Magnus continuing toward the center of town. With every tube transfer he felt the flow grow stronger, as though he were wandering upstream into the tumultuous rapids of a river. Every fourth house or so was replaced by an internet café or bookstore, then the houses began inching closer together, blocks interrupted by restaurants, then apartment buildings, and finally no place to live at all, just businesses with lit-up signs and wares on display. Men and women conducted conversations on hands-free phones, speaking into buds dangling from their ears, weaving from hydrant to hydrant, intersections turning into cat's cradles of tubing that miraculously resolved with every light change. Magnus rarely made it this far into town, and he couldn't tell if it was his own excitement or his proximity to the gigantic energy-giving organ that made him feel as though he were being hit in the chest with a fire hose. He stopped and leaned against the front of a bagel shop. When the owner told him to get lost, he turned into an alley, hurrying past a couple junkies shooting up directly into their vein tubes. Luckily, the detoxification department would scrub the drugs from the blood when it returned to the kidney section of the plant.

Magnus changed into his grandfather's uniform behind a dumpster. It was clearly too big for him. How would anyone be fooled? He'd be found out, tossed into jail, left to die of lethal disattachment on death row. Then he imagined the swaying palms of Beverly Hills, the witty people in pastel sweaters, and it was enough to propel him forward, onto the sidewalk, toward the decrepit former cathedral that served as the plant's main point of entrance.

The cathedral's exterior was all sooty stone and busted stained-glass windows. One of its spires had crumbled long after the god worshipped here had been forgotten. Workers in uniforms like Ike's hurried in and out of the opening where the doors used to be, trailing tubes, great red ropes of speeding blood. Magnus fell into a mass of workers on their way to their shifts. Inside the cathedral, the workers branched off toward various banks of escalators marked with different departments: Aorta, Left Ventricle, Right Ventricle, Pulmonary Vessels, Mitral Valve. There didn't appear to be any sign for the tumor farm, so Magnus headed toward the elevator leading to the Left Ventricle, where his grandfather had worked.

"Hey, hold it a minute there, son." A security officer of some sort grabbed Magnus by the shoulder. He had a big blond mustache and wore the heart-shaped insignia of the plant on his chest, with all the chambers highlighted in green to indicate he had full access. "You're obviously new here. You can't go in with these wimpy surgical tubes; they can't stand the pressure. You'll need to go to the Bypass office and get some new ones. And whoever issued you this uniform, they must have been in a real retro mood. Let them know you're going to need new duds."

"Where is the Bypass office?" Magnus said.

"Man, you are green. Up there." The officer pointed to a place high above the floor, a kind of balcony just out of reach of the pipe organ. Magnus took the appropriately labeled elevator and exited into an office overlooking the throng of workers below. Administrative types wearing shirts and ties hurried about, making photocopies, faxing spreadsheets. A woman at a broad ebony desk motioned for Magnus to have a seat, telling him she'd be with him after she completed an email. A minute or two later, she turned and said, "So. First day. We're glad you're here, Magnus. We've been looking forward to your arrival since your grandfather retired. You'll find that around here he's a real legend. You'll need new tubes, a new uniform, a real ID card." Magnus plugged into a nearby outlet that sent blood coursing so powerfully into his body that he felt he could climb a mountain and filled out some paperwork.

That day Magnus was put to work in the outskirts of the vast underground operation, monitoring flow to and from the poorer neighborhoods. Someday, his shift supervisor, Jim, told him, he could work his way up from these dank subterranean passages to work on an actual valve, maybe even the Purkinje fibers. His grandfather had started out at the bottom of the totem pole, repairing capillaries. Through hard work he had become one of the most respected valvemen this operation had ever had the honor of employing.

For the first weeks of his employment, Magnus walked for miles under the city, pressing his stethoscope against the pipes through which oxygenated blood flowed, noting changes in pressure in his palm computer, and calling in the repair crew whenever he detected a leak. Magnus learned to locate leaks by following rats and other misshapen vermin who could smell the blood before any human. One morning Magnus followed a gaggle of rats down several flights of stairs and came upon an entrance to the tumor farm. The space was as big as a stadium, the floor, walls, and ceiling high overhead covered in strange fleshy forms that almost resembled trees. The floor was rubbery down here, and occasionally viscous fluids squirted up from underfoot like clams spitting on a beach. While the handbook had assured Magnus that nothing in the tumor farm was contagious, the place still put him ill at ease. He swept his Maglite across the trembling mounds of flesh, each grotesque growth fueled by the same blood that beat quickly in his own body.

"You lost, kid?" said a man perched on a tumor in the vague shape of a couch. He wore the insignia of his department on his dirty jumpsuit next to his name, Kyle, and a cap drawn low over his eyes. He picked his fingernails with a knife. Magnus hurriedly introduced himself and explained he had come here following rats, but this didn't provoke any change in the bored expression fixed on Kyle's face.

"I'm looking for someone named Gatton, who worked with my grandfather Ike. My grandfather said Gatton could help me."

Kyle nodded and motioned for Magnus to follow him. They wound their way through a forest of abnormal growths. "We keep this tumor farm for a reason, in case you hadn't figured it out by now," Kyle said. "For years we been trying to develop individual hearts for folks to carry around in they own chests, not bein' dependent on the big thumper up there in the cave. Down here's where the cardiac scientists cultivate materials and toss their failed experiments. When the breakthrough comes, we'll be turning this place into a giant factory of hearts, with the people coming in one end empty-chested and leaving the other with independent tickers allowing them to not have to hook up to the blood hydrants every goddamn day. Then we can destroy that big muscle that keeps us all enslaved to the ebb and flow."

They found a slippery staircase and made their way down deep enough for Magnus to have to pop his ears. Finally the stairs opened into an echoing chamber that was more vast than the tumor farm and reeked of blood. As Magnus's eyes adjusted, he came to understand that he was standing on the bank of an underground river of blood, too wide to see across to the other shore.

"They'll come soon enough," Kyle said, taking off his hat, wiping his brow. As if lying in wait, the sounds of a vessel came across the flowing plasma, ringing with percussion and horns. From the dark emerged a craft about forty feet long. At first Magnus thought the people crowded on its deck were men in armored suits, but slowly they revealed themselves to be birds the size of humans, standing upright, some of them wearing jeweled clothes or helmets, squawking hideously with their long beaks.

"I wasn't supposed to see this place yet," Magnus said, though the words seemed as foreign in his mouth as the creatures before him. He couldn't help feeling that some sealed repository of knowledge had been opened within his mind, some place that had existed prior to his birth, now revealed on the path his curiosity had so dangerously compelled him to follow. The bird beings in their craft raised a great squawking din of horns and drums upon seeing him standing petrified on the shore, a sound panicked and angry, and this was enough to frighten Magnus back up the stairs to the tumor farm, into the labyrinth of vessel-lined halls, and out an exit into the night of a town he no longer understood.

Magnus tried to cleanse himself of the disturbing scene he had witnessed by throwing himself into his routines. That night was movie night with his grandfather. He chose a video at the video store and walked across the park in the middle of town with it tucked under his arm, a bag of burritos from his favorite taqueria in the other. He decided the only way to relieve his fear of the bird creatures on the river of blood was to convince himself that they had been a hallucination. By the time he reached his grandfather's house, he had decided that he must have been working too hard these past few weeks and suffered a fatigue-related mental lapse. This idea comforted him, more so than the possibility that there existed beneath his feet an underground blood river navigated by alien forms.

If he had peeked in the windows when he arrived at his grandfather's house, Magnus would have certainly noticed something awfully wrong about the place. But instead he instinctively grabbed the doorknob and entered without knocking, as was his habit. Instead of being met with Ike's friendly hello, a wall of blood swept Magnus off the porch, depositing him in the gnarled rosebushes in the front lawn. He'd heard of this problem before but had never seen it actually happen. A leak that slowly fills an entire house. Waves of the red stuff rolled out to the street. Inside he found the entire place awash in blood, covering every surface, saturating every permeable material. He rushed to his grandfather's bedroom, where he found the drowned body still in bed, unrecognizable, covered in all this mess. Crying, he carried the body from the house.

After the ambulance arrived, leisurely, with its sirens off, Magnus sat in the blood-soaked front lawn watching night crawlers emerge from the tunnels hidden beneath the grass. Some police officers may have spoken to him; he couldn't be sure. As the light faded and the seizure crew exited the house, Magnus felt a hand on his shoulder and looked up to see Carly in her plaid pants, holding a suitcase.

"It's time to leave this place," Carly said.

"I think there's only one way to leave this place," Magnus said. "And it's underground. At least until they start manufacturing individual hearts."

Carly opened her suitcase, moved aside some shirts and showed him the two mechanical hearts inside. They were made of bright-yellow plastic, like waterproof electronic equipment.

The Guy Who Kept Meeting Himself

PETER STARTED MEETING OLDER VERSIONS OF HIMSELF WHEN HE WAS SIX YEARS OLD.

He was sitting on a bench in front of the library waiting for his mother to pick him up when a twelve-year-old sat beside him. The boy looked like he could have been Peter's older brother, but in fact it was Peter himself, years later. He wore a cool jean jacket, and his hair was styled in a mullet.

"What's up?" older Peter said.

"I got a book about spiders," younger Peter said.

And that was about the extent of the conversation because younger Peter's mom arrived. She didn't notice the older, shaggier version of her own son.

A few years passed and Peter was fifteen, hanging out in a mall food court, drinking a blackberry milk shake. A twenty-five-year-old version of himself sat down. Young Peter thought about the first time he'd met an older version of himself and how he had blown the chance to ask him questions about the future. This time he was prepared.

"When do I lose my virginity?" young Peter said.

"You sure you wanna know?"

"Yeah."

"Third year of college, October 12, 1991."

Young Peter was so disappointed with the answer he forgot to ask any other questions.

Sure enough, when October 12, 1991, rolled around, Peter finally convinced a girl to sleep with him. They ended up getting married after graduation and having two kids in quick succession. Peter put his electrical engineering degree to work as a computer programmer. It was hard work, but he made a lot of money in the tech boom. Still he suspected that true happiness eluded him. By the time another future self paid him a visit he had a six-bedroom house and three cars. The future self was forty-one. He walked up to Peter one morning while younger Peter was stretching for his daily jog. They looked fairly similar, though older Peter had less hair and a thicker middle.

"Spend more time with your kids," older Peter said.

"Easy for you to say," younger Peter said, then asked his older self for any hot stock tips.

"You sure you want to know?" the older man said.

"Of course I'm sure."

The older self obliged with some names of companies that didn't exist yet. In coming years Peter would make out big with his investments. He'd buy a vacation house in Hawaii, which was where he sat one afternoon at age forty-five enjoying the sunset when a sixty-two year-old man appeared who was unmistakably himself.

"Hey, it's you again," said younger Peter. "Say, my wife just found a lump on her breast. Is she going to be all right?"

"You really want to know?"

"Yeah."

"The lump is irrelevant because your wife is going to die in a car accident next year," older Peter said. "And there's nothing you can do to prevent it."

"Way to make my day," younger Peter said. In the following year—the worst year of his life so far—he did everything he could to prevent his wife from riding in cars. One night before Christmas he let his guard down, and she got into a car with her sister, who was visiting from New York. They were hit by a drunk driver, and Peter's wife died instantly.

The kids went to college and Peter retired, living more or less permanently in his vacation home on the beach. Even though he'd become a very wealthy man, he regretted never living in the moment and had come to hate his future selves for ruining all his surprises—good and bad. So when, at the age of sixty-seven, he met his eighty-year-old self, he was prepared.

"When am I going to die?" he asked his older self, slowly reaching for a revolver hidden under a towel.

"You really want to know?"

"Yes, yes I do."

"Right about now," the older Peter said sadly, stabbing the younger Peter in the chest with a knife he'd been hiding in his dungarees.

As younger Peter died, he looked up at his older self and whispered, "But I was going to kill you."

The older Peter shook his head.

"I COULD HAVE TOLD YOU IT WASN'T GOING TO HAPPEN LIKE THAT."

Bleeding Man and Wounded Deer

Man, I had so many stab wounds, it was crazy.

There I was at the conference center, and I hadn't even adequately prepared my remarks. At the registration booth the ladies looked at me, trying to hide their disgust, but managed to hand me my lanyard and orientation packet without barfing. I was dressed pretty nice, too, with a new Façonnable shirt and my favorite jacket. I thought I looked pretty good despite the blood spurting from eight places on my torso. But I had a presentation to give, people to drink with and share stories with, and a whole binder full of notes I needed to process sometime between breakout sessions.

Practically seconds after slipping the lanyard around my neck, which was also gushing blood in two places, I was sideswiped by my old colleague Nick, who immediately laid down an elongated "Heeey!" and asked me how the hell I'd been.

"Fantastic, Nick, yourself?"

"Can't complain. You look like you lost weight since I saw you—what was it? Six months ago?"

I tried to make a joke, saying, "Well, with all this blood I'm losing, I'm sure I'm still losing weight."

Nick looked at the floor and seemed a little embarrassed or put off by the remark. People get uneasy when you point out the elephant in the room. "Yeah, well. Say, I'm totally looking forward to your preso. I'll be there in the front row, buddy."

"You take care, Nick."

Blood had trickled from the wounds on my groin and thighs, down my legs, and into my shoes. The shoes made a squishy sound now that I was really hoping no one would notice, but I didn't have time to run up to my room to change them before the opening reception. While some of my colleagues eye-rolled the contrived meet-and-greet atmospherics of that particular mixer, I'd always appreciated the opportunity to grab a glass of wine and chat with the newcomers. When I got to the reception, the front of my shirt was saturated through. Still everyone smiled and gave me hugs, even though my blood was getting all over everything. Their clothes, the floor, the wads of napkins I kept pressing to the various lacerations.

Rachel, with whom I go way back to when we were both junior account reps, greeted me warmly, careful not to spill her plastic cup of merlot, then muttered, "I heard what happened. You holding up okay?"

"Yeah, no, I'm fine," I said. "How are the kids?"

"Seriously, dude. You should have yourself some 'you' time right now."

"That's kind of you to say," I said. "I'm kinda hungry. Is the cheese plate any good?"

Rachel sniffed. "Gouda's just a slutted-up Velveeta in my opinion."

And then I had to catch up with Ross, and with Mike, and found myself roped into joining Pat, Yukio, and Dennis at the hotel bar, where we played many rounds of a game called Kill, Marry, or Fuck. It works like this: you're given three names of people—famous people or people you know personally—and you have to decide which of them you'd kill, which you'd marry, and which you'd fuck. Hours and expense reports can get eaten up while playing this game.

I was so exhausted (I'd traveled that morning, too, I remembered) that I blew off my notes and just collapsed in bed late that night. When I woke the next morning, the sheets looked dyed, like I intended to use them as theater curtains. I felt bad for the housekeeping staff.

But dammit, I had a presentation to give. I showered and changed even though I knew I'd wreck my new change of clothes, which I promptly did. I guess changing into a more formal outfit is kind of a psychological thing, a boost before a performance. Checking myself in the mirror, I said, "You're going to go out there and blow their minds, my friend. Go take what is rightfully yours."

And I have to say, as far as my presentation went, I killed it. From beginning to end I had the audience's attention, had them laughing at all the right parts, and at the end they rose to their feet as one and delivered a standing ovation, seeming to ignore the fact that I was standing in a puddle of my own plasma.

And as I was presenting, looking out at that hotel ballroom audience, I spotted, among my old friends and new acquaintances, a doe, sitting in an aisle seat, attentively listening and batting her dark doe eyes. I kept looking at her, finding her incredibly beautiful. She clutched a little handbag between her doe hooves. After the thunderous applause had died down and been replaced by chuckles and chatter, I pulled aside a good friend of mine, Matthew, and asked him what the deal was with the female deer in attendance. As I asked, I scanned the room but couldn't find her.

Matthew shrugged. "Word is that not long ago she was hit by a car. Why, you like her?"

"She's just so… interesting," I said.

"Well, she's going to be at the prefunc mixer in an hour, or at least she was invited, if you're into it."

Of course I was into it. An hour later I squished my way through the hotel lobby to another, smaller, more intimate ballroom, where a jazz trio played as unobtrusively as a meek junior-high math teacher asking his students to set down their pencils. And there she was, the doe, the light from a mirror ball overhead playing with the sun-dappled coloration of her coat. I so wanted to make out with her.

But, you know, recognizing that we were different species and not knowing how she'd react to the tremendous volume of blood spurting out of me, I hung back a bit, tried to casually catch her eye from across the room. It didn't seem to be working, or she was purposely ignoring me; it was hard to tell. Finally, as the mixer began to clear out, I saw she wasn't conversing with anyone, just checking for texts on her phone, and so I sidled up and introduced myself. She nodded and said, "I'm Angela. Boy, you really rocked that presentation today."

Downplaying, I said, "It's a miracle I didn't blow any lines."

And wouldn't you know it, just then something shifted in me and I vomited blood all over that wounded deer's chest fur.

"I am so, so sorry," I said.

"No, it's quite okay," Angela said, searching her handbag for an inadequate facial tissue. "That's to be expected, given your state."

"I heard you got hit by a car," I said. "Sounds like a bummer."

"Oh yeah," she said. "I may look like I have it all together, but on the inside I'm a train wreck."

I found myself desperately wanting to fix that train wreck. I'm no veterinarian, but I'm a good listener, and for a moment I believed I could help her. "I want to help you," I said. "I want to be here for you."

Before she could respond, Matthew and Rachel swooped in and said, "We were looking for you, pal!" and "Dude, you've been going nonstop since who knows when."

So I let them walk me back to my room, where I again collapsed on my bed, which had been turned down, and I didn't even have the energy to eat the complimentary chocolate.

I watched the doe from afar for the rest of the conference, realizing I'd totally blown it. I should've waited until I had a chance to get sewed up first before I even approached her. The last thing a wounded deer needs is some human fountain vomiting blood on her. I'd overstepped, and I wouldn't be surprised if that beautiful creature never wanted to talk to me again.

By the third day of the conference, I was bled dry. I'd never not had blood in my body, but the sensation was as you'd expect—cold, dry, like becoming a human ghost town.

I WAS STANDING IN THE AISLE on page 238 of Doris Kearns Goodwin's *Team of Rivals* when a guy tapped me on the arm. Heavyset, looked my age, shaved head, slightly tinted glasses, walrus mustache. He held up his copy of the same book.

"Funny," I said. "What page are you on?"

"Just got to 239."

We had a laugh over this. The Republican National Convention of 1860 was getting underway, and soon it would be my stop. Before I hopped off, I told him my name was Phillip. He said his name was Marty.

"This your usual route?" I said.

"Sure is. I'll be on it tomorrow."

"Maybe by then we'll know whether Abe got the nomination," I said. Ten minutes later I was in spreadsheet land.

THE NEXT MORNING I spotted Marty again and gave him a little chin-thrust hello. In the weeks that followed neither of us got much reading done on the bus. Without either of us planning it, we formed a book group of two, joking about humorless Secretary of War Edwin Stanton and the unpretentious Ulysses S. Grant. Over the couple weeks that Marty and I were both reading *Team of Rivals*, neither of us asked the other about jobs or family. We were just two guys immersed in the intrigues of the sixteenth president's cabinet. I looked forward to these conversations and would come home and tell my wife, Shel, about Marty's observations. Having no real interest in history, particularly Civil War history, she nodded politely and indulged me in my nightly reports.

Then, over the course of a long weekend, I finished the book. I prowled the bookshelves in my study for an acceptable volume to follow Kearns Goodwin, settling on one of the DeLillo novels I hadn't read yet, *The Names*.

Here's where it got weird.

When I stepped on the bus the following Tuesday, I spotted Marty right away, sitting in one of the higher seats above the wheel well, absorbed in *The Names* by Don DeLillo. Same edition even.

We had another laugh over this. What were the chances? He told me he'd been saving *The Names* for some time, having been a fan of DeLillo since he was a teenager. Me too, I confided. The conversation turned to other books. Suddenly it was like my head had turned inside out. Every book I mentioned, he had read. And every book he mentioned, I had read. I rattled off *The Complete Works of Isaac Babel*, Heaney's translation of *Beowulf*, Aimee Bender's *Willful Creatures*, Camus's *The Plague*. He nodded at each title. He threw me Stephen King's *The Stand*, Murakami's *Hard-Boiled Wonderland and the End of the World*, Kurzweil's *The Singularity Is Near*. Yep, I'd read those, too. I missed my stop. I countered with René Daumal's *Mount Analogue*, Bolaño's *2666*, Victoria Nelson's *The Secret Life of Puppets*, and our current president's *The Audacity of Hope*. Sure enough, he'd read them, too. We exchanged email addresses. I got off at his stop, walked back to my office, got chewed out by my boss. The reprimand didn't dent me, though. I was in some kind of Borgesian haze, having just met my readerly equal.

W HEN I GOT HOME THAT NIGHT and told Shel, she didn't believe me. "One of you must have been lying," she said. "You couldn't have possibly read all the same books."

"I'm not making this up. *He* might have been bullshitting, sure, but every book he mentioned was something I've read. We're both reading *The Names!*"

Shel yawned. "We've got two *Mad Men*s on the DVR. Want to open the new cabernet and watch them with me?"

That night after Shel fell asleep, I tossed in bed thinking of books I'd read, the more obscure the better. Danilo Kiš's essay collection *Homo Poeticus*. Gary Lutz's chapbook *Partial List of People to Bleach*. Michel Houellebecq's *H.P. Lovecraft: Against the World, Against Life*. Stuff only a literary nerd like myself would really get cranked up about.

I decided to send Marty an email and got out of bed. When I opened my inbox, I found he'd beaten me to it. His email contained fifty or so titles. There was David Lynch's *Catching the Big Fish*, Barthelme's *Sixty Stories*, books by Pynchon, Mutis, Hempel, and Márquez. Whether it was fiction or nonfiction, it didn't matter. Each was a title I'd read. Who has read Ryū Murakami's *Almost Transparent Blue*? Who has read Halldór Laxness's *World Light*? Or Trinie Dalton's *Wide Eyed*? Plenty of people, I suppose, but how many people have read all three of them?

I countered with a list of my own. Thomas Bernhard's *The Lime Works*. Georges Perec's *A Void*. *Rock Springs* by Richard Ford. J. K. Huysmans's *Là-bas*. A book-length critical essay by D. X. Ferris about Slayer's classic thrash-metal album *Reign in Blood*.

"I have to see your library," I wrote to Marty.

"Likewise," he replied, more or less instantly. We made a date of it. I'd stop by his place the following night around seven.

MARTY CAUGHT THE BUS just one stop before mine, and as the crow flies his house was probably no more than a half mile from my own. I lived on one side of the hill facing the lake, with a view of

Mount Rainier, and he lived on the other side within spitting distance of a Jiffy Lube. His place was an awkward Spanish-style bungalow painted kelly green with an unweeded front yard held in place by a crotch-high chain-link fence. He opened the door and offered me a beer. It was pretty obvious right away he lived by himself. The furnishings were slim. In the kitchen, it appeared the microwave oven was pulling all the weight. Maybe he'd made an attempt at tidying up before I arrived, then run out of time. The dinette table had been half-wiped with a wet washcloth that sat crumpled next to a napkin dispenser probably stolen from a restaurant. The living room was lined with his shelves.

If there had been books I had not read I would have been disappointed, but the mystery of our perfectly aligned reading tastes persisted as I ran my eyes along the spines. Turns out Marty did own books I hadn't read, but these were books he hadn't read, either. It finally dawned on me that there was a Corona with lime in my hand. I settled into the room's only chair, a nice oxblood leather one, and tried to express my amazement.

"I can't explain it, either," Marty said, scratching his chin. "It's like those stories you hear about twins separated at birth, the ones who meet each other as adults and discover they've both married women named Pam and both drive Dodge Dakotas."

"So you must have been an English major or something, right?" I said.

Marty nodded. "Graduated from Boston College in 1995."

"I went to Evergreen. Also graduated in '95. Then grad school. Bennington, creative writing."

"I did the Warren Wilson program," Marty said.

"I'm being set up here, right? Tell me this is some kind of weird reality show thing."

Marty shrugged. "I'm just as blown away about this as you are. By the way, I started rereading one of my favorite books today."

"*Jesus' Son*, right?" I said.

Marty nodded and finished his beer in a gulp. I stayed till eleven, getting drunk, talking about books that had changed our lives. We went way back, through high school's Bukowski and Kosiński and Kerouac jags, junior high's fascination with paramilitary potboilers and Stephen King doorstoppers, then grade school's Newbery award winners and Tintin comics. By the time I left, we'd exhausted *The Poky Little Puppy*, *The Summerfolk*, *The Great*

Brain, and *The Sneetches and Other Stories.* I gave Marty a man hug at the front door and invited him over for dinner the following week.

B Y THE TIME MARTY CAME OVER, we'd been having a week-long discussion about Denis Johnson and the current book we happened to be reading at the same time, *Moby-Dick.*

As it turned out, that night wasn't so great for Shel; she'd had to lay off twelve employees that day. She arrived home needing to cry it out with a couple glasses of wine and some *Colbert Report* to bring herself down a few notches, but instead she had to put on a social face and entertain this new weird friend of mine she'd never met.

When Marty walked in the door I knew how he must have looked to Shel. He wasn't grotesque by any means, but he could have used a shave, and the Top Pot Doughnuts T-shirt he wore looked like it had been recycled a few times. I don't think Marty expected me to live in the kind of house he walked into. Shel and I had done pretty well for ourselves in the ten years since our wedding, and when we finally decided to own a home, we got a screaming deal on a recently remodeled four-bedroom, three-story house in a neighborhood where the trees had been shading the sidewalks since before cars existed.

Marty complimented our place, and we did a little dance about whether or not he should take off his shoes in the foyer. Shel appeared at the top of the stairs in a new blouse and her pearls and warmly greeted our visitor. After some awkward small talk, I asked Marty if he wanted to see my books.

My study was about the size of his living room, the bookcases custom built.

"How strange we've come together like this," Marty said, touching the spines.

A while later we ate pizzas made with homemade dough and drank the last of a case of something Shel and I had picked up from a winery tour of Lake Chelan. I tried pulling Shel into the conversation, but as soon as I shared some meaningless literary matter Marty and I had wrestled over, it became apparent how thoroughly unengaged she was. Marty tried to involve her by asking about her job, not realizing that this was perhaps the absolute worst day for such a question. After an acceptable period of time, Shel excused herself for the night, apologetically blaming a long day and an early meeting the next morning. Which was true.

After Shel left, Marty said, "So do you still write?"

"You mean after I got my MFA? Well, I mean, I try once in a while. I'm just so busy. What about you?"

Marty shrugged. "I've got this novel I've been working on."

"How long have you been at it?"

"About fourteen, fifteen years."

"Damn! You must be pretty far into it by now."

Marty looked at the floor. "I suppose I am," he said quietly.

"How many pages?"

He shrugged. "Fifteen hundred or so."

"Shit, Marty."

He must have known what I desperately wanted to ask next, because he cut me off at the pass. "It's not ready for anyone to read yet. It still needs some work."

"Do you have a title?"

"Yeah. *The Dystopians*."

"I'd definitely read it with a title like that."

"Yeah, well, it's not ready." Marty threw his gaze around the room at potted plants and framed art. "That was one excellent dinner, my friend," he said, slapping his knee. "I shouldn't keep you guys up." He checked his watch. "The 106 hasn't stopped running yet, has it?"

"Hey, no, let me drive you."

Marty waved me off. "It might seem like far away, but it's just over the hill. I can walk if there's no bus. Serious. Tell Shel I really enjoyed her company."

A WEEK PASSED IN WHICH I DIDN'T SEE MARTY on the bus. I emailed him a few times, writing, "So I assume you're reading Diane Williams's *Excitability*?" and "Dude, I hope you're okay."

Work rose up and swallowed me for awhile. Long nights putting out fires, the rumor mill at full churn about layoffs, accounts diving overboard: plenty of occasions that warranted mixed metaphors. When I finally had the wherewithal to think about books again, I popped into one of my favorite used bookstores while on a lunch break and found my fingers resting on a battered copy of *On Death and Dying* by Elisabeth Kübler-Ross. I'd always wanted to read it, and at two bucks it was a steal. As I began reading on the bus home, I knew I had to pay Marty a visit. When I showed up at his house that night, I found the lights out. I knocked on and off for five minutes, peered in windows, and figured he wasn't home.

Two days later I felt the compulsion to read the Bible and knew that Marty must have been in really bad shape. I started calling hospitals, but here's the thing—I'd never bothered to learn Marty's last name. I wouldn't get anywhere asking the front desk if they'd admitted a voracious reader named Marty.

At work, my face remained friendly and strained, scaffolded by my contrived persona as an enthusiastic manager of projects. Shel put on her own brave face as her direct reports clamored for reassurance that they wouldn't be next on the gallows. She had to look many of them in the eye and outright lie that their jobs weren't in danger. When Shel and I came home, these faces collapsed and various sites of domestic insignificance became the triggers for raging arguments. I forgot to buy more dishwasher soap. Shel neglected to tell me my mother had called. We clashed, exhausted ourselves, fell into one another's arms with Jon Stewart mugging on the flat screen.

I emailed Marty. "What's with all the religious texts?" I wrote. "Just tell me you're okay."

Finally I got a reply. It just said, "Sorry I've been incommunicado. Things not well. I need to see you."

I walked into his house without knocking that night and found him in bed in a little room stinking of boxed-in sweat. Beside him on the floor and bedside table were copies of all the books I'd been reading for the past couple weeks, spread eagled and marked up with margin notes.

"I'm dying," he said. "I don't have anybody. My family lives in other states."

"You need a hospital," I said.

Marty shook his head. "Three months ago they said I had two months."

I sat on the edge of the bed and held his hand. "Three months ago was when we met," I said.

Marty swallowed and swallowing appeared to hurt. "I need you to finish the manuscript." His eyes led mine to a cardboard box partially obscured by a shirt. Inside I found several reams' worth of paper covered with Times New Roman size 10. He said, "Remember that part in the Lincoln book, before he became famous, where he told his friend he didn't want to die without anybody knowing he'd ever lived? That's what this manuscript is to me. But I can't finish it. You're the only one who can."

"Marty, I don't know."

"You dropped your writing as soon as you got out of grad school. But you kept reading. My novel will fill the hole you created when you set aside your own work."

"You need to see a doctor."

"I need to die surrounded by books. Read something to me. Read me Carver's 'Cathedral.'"

I found the Library of America edition of the *Collected Stories* and sat on the floor next to the bed. I read about the husband and the wife and the blind man. By the time the wife went to bed, Marty was asleep. By the time the husband guided the blind man's hands across the paper, Marty was dead.

MY LIFE WOULDN'T LET ME STOP to process this strange tragedy; the very next day I lost my job. I called Shel from the bus on my way home, and she arranged to get out of work for the rest of the day. She found me in the living room staring at the two cardboard boxes sitting on the coffee table, one containing Marty's novel, the other containing Mariners bobbleheads, vacation snapshots, HR paperwork, and the bottle of champagne I'd kept for five years in a file cabinet. I had two months' severance. Shel pulled up Microsoft Money on her laptop and charted our finances—things wouldn't start getting hairy for at least a year.

THERE WAS A FUNERAL TO ATTEND. I met Marty's relatives, who hailed from various places in the Midwest. Affable people who didn't read books. They watched TV shows and played video games. They excitedly retold a story about their cab ride from the airport that didn't seem all that noteworthy to me. I told them how insightful their son, their cousin, their brother had been. Their expressions told me that they felt obligated to come across as friendly. Reading wasn't important to them, wasn't something necessary for their survival, and in fact probably would have complicated it. Once again I found myself understanding that this was how most people were these days. I didn't mention Marty's and my perfectly synchronized reading habits or that he'd written a novel. One of them, an uncle, owned a car dealership and kept offering me gum. Another, an aunt, kept repeating the phrase "weird little kid" when talking about Marty. None seemed to have any clue that he'd been a writer.

The day after the funeral, I started reading the novel. Hours previous I had looked upon my friend laid out waxy and inert in a coffin, and yet the man never seemed as alive to me as when I read the words he'd committed to those pages. I had to stop several times to weep, and immediately after reading the last sentence, I slipped the thumb drive he'd given me into my laptop and started editing the soft copy. Nothing drastic, of course—just a typo fixed here and some untangled syntax there. The more I got my hands in it, the more the novel's subtexts called attention to themselves and the more glaring its flaws became. It was as though all the books I'd read had been precisely what I needed to prepare me for this task, finishing and editing one of the most brilliant works of literature of our time. I began to see exactly what this novel needed to become truly great, and spent my days deleting and adding the passages it required.

My wife got up early, went to work, came home exhausted. I barely noticed her comings and goings. I diligently submitted my unemployment claims and had to go to an acupuncturist when my hands grew too sore from typing. On the anniversary of Marty's death, I came to the end of my work on *Utopia's Garden* (I'd changed the title) and began looking for an agent. After a bit of googling, I came up with a list of addresses and drafted my query letter. I had just finished writing my first novel, I told them, and I was seeking representation.

I.

A room lit by a bank of monitors. Two technicians,
Ross and Andy, watch the progress of the subjects.
If the subjects perform outside the performance
parameters, there are a number of contingency strategies in the Standard Operating Procedures (SOP)
manual to which Ross and Andy must refer.

Ross and Andy are males between the ages of
twenty-five and forty. Both wear the codified
uniforms of their positions as technicians. They
intently watch the subjects who are themselves
performing monitoring activities, observing the

activities of certain sub-subjects. It is difficult for Ross and Andy to make out the activities of these sub-subjects, as Ross and Andy do not have direct access to what their own subjects are watching on their (the subjects') monitors. Not that Ross and Andy haven't tried. They have squinted and pressed their noses against their monitors trying to make out what the sub-subjects are doing on the monitors their subjects are viewing.

Occasionally one of the subjects violates their Personal Performance Parameters and Ross and Andy must refer to the SOPs for the appropriate contingency strategy. These contingencies consist solely of referring to the appropriate escalation pathway and submitting an alert, after which corrective action is taken. When corrective action is taken, the monitor displaying the subject in question goes blank, or is supposed to. Ross and Andy have postulated that their equipment needs replacing because occasionally the monitor view has been left on while a particular corrective action is taking place. Corrective actions can be as simple as a Corrective Referee visiting the subject and talking to them a short while or perhaps giving them some medicine. Twice Ross and Andy have witnessed a Corrective Referee discipline a subject with violence. They have never seen outright termination, but they have seen restored monitor views showing just an empty, disheveled room, and in one case a custodian cleaning a bloody handprint off a wall.

Ross thinks these sightings are accidental, but Andy has a theory that they have been purposely shown the outcome of their taking the appropriate contingency strategy with regard to their subjects performing outside their Personal Performance Parameters. Andy is of the opinion that being able to infer the nature of a more intense kind of corrective action has made them Ross and Andy better performers.

Ross finds this hard to believe, and notes that they aren't even being observed.

Andy challenges Ross on this point. How does Ross know they are not being observed?

Ross notes that they certainly have never had a visit from a Corrective Referee, which would prove that they were being monitored.

Exactly, Andy says, because they have never deviated from their Personal Performance Parameters. So the only way to determine whether they are being observed is to violate them.

Ross thinks this is a ridiculous plan and refuses to go along with it. Andy says that Ross secretly believes he is being observed and is afraid of corrective action, that he has spent countless hours in this room soldering in his mind a connection between deviating from the Parameters and receiving correction. But if they are not being observed, as Ross claims, they have nothing to fear.

So Andy reaches out and turns off a monitor. They have watched their subjects perform this very action, for which they received stern words from

Corrective Referees. Ross asks Andy to turn the monitor back on. An argument ensues, and perhaps driven
by boredom, Ross struggles with Andy physically and
strikes him with his fist, then turns the monitor
back on. Andy slowly rises from the floor, wiping
blood off his lip, and makes a pointed comment about
how Ross would make a great Corrective Referee.

A few minutes pass wordlessly as they observe the
subjects on their monitors. Then there is a knock
on the door and both technicians jump, startled.
They typically actually never get visitors. Andy
opens the door and the Corrective Referee appears,
seemingly proving Andy's theory. He wears the suit
and the tidy hair of all Corrective Referees, and
his tie is decorated with little cartoon characters.

There are only two chairs in the place, so Andy yields his and leans against the table their monitors sit on. It is meant to be a casual posture, but his arms are crossed and it is clear he is having troubling thoughts.   °

   Say, the Corrective Referee says, I know things can get a little uncomfortable here with the close quarters and all. You fellows have a real tough job, and hey, it's only human that from time to time nerves get frayed. I'm here to help. So say, tell you what, I've got a couple cards with entertainment codes I'd like to give you. Here, take them, use them in your rooms tonight. You know, relax. I understand there's a great batch of new releases. And if you need anything else, feel free to contact me per the appropriate contingencies. Buck up. You guys are doing a fabulous job.

The Corrective Referee leaves and seems to take with him whatever animosity Ross and Andy shared in that brief, explosive moment. It goes without saying that they are indeed being observed, though via what means it's hard to surmise. They survey the walls and ceiling, trying not to be conspicuous, knowing they are being observed in the act of trying to determine how they're being observed. Ultimately, the technology is too sophisticated for them to detect. What would come of finding the miniature cameras, anyway? If they were to locate them and obscure them, they would certainly be violating the their own Personal Performance Parameters.

The end of their shift finally comes, and both technicians retreat to their private rooms, eat, and enter their respective entertainment codes. Andy settles on an entertainment in which the righteous prevail and the wicked are vanquished swiftly and without prejudice. Ross watches an entertainment about a big dog and how it disrupts one family's routines with hilarious results.

Both technicians return to their work space the next day with their coffees and pastries and proceed to monitor their subjects. Ross, feeling horrible about the previous day's outburst, apologizes to Andy. Andy mumbles something noncommittal in response, and for the better part of the day, they don't speak to one another.

A little after lunch, Ross spots a violation on monitor four. One of the subjects is violently smashing his own monitors with the base of his swivel chair.

Ross says, I believe that's a section seven violation right there. He taps the screen with a pen. Andy sits doing nothing but watching the monitor, so Ross takes it upon himself to report the incident. A few minutes later the monitor goes into standby mode. The Corrective Referee has no doubt paid his visit to their subject.

This is bullshit, Andy says. You and I are both one centimeter from doing exactly what that subject just did.

You're talking crazy, Ross says.

I'm crazy? You're the one who brained me yesterday, don't you remember?

Yeah, I remember. And for the second time today, I apologize. Whatever mood you're in doesn't justify neglecting your monitoring responsibilities.

Bullshit, Andy says again. He pauses a moment before an expression of surprise passes over him, as if something he once knew but had forgotten has been revealed anew. He stands, walks from the room, and doesn't return the rest of his shift.

Ross smolders throughout the rest of the day. Not only does he have to monitor twice as many monitors as he usually does, but he also suspects that his inability to keep Andy focused on his tasks will reflect poorly on his own performance.

He performs as best he can, and that night in bed he falls into a forest of nightmares.

The following morning Andy is already in his seat when Ross arrives. He doesn't look good. He appears fatigued, and there's a bandage over one of his eyebrows. He hasn't touched his coffee or pastry. His eyes move from one monitor to the next, but Ross can't tell if he's actually processing what he's seeing. The only way to find out is to wait until one of the subjects on Andy's monitors violates a Performance Parameter. Ross again performs double monitoring duty, just in case. Mid-morning he notices one of Andy's subjects slumped in a sleeping position in his chair. Apparently Andy doesn't notice, so Ross scoots his chair over and submits the alert using Andy's keyboard. As the subject on the monitor is being visited by a Corrective Referee bearing a pot of black coffee, the door to Ross and Andy's workspace opens and their own Corrective Referee appears, his shirtsleeves rolled up and his tie loosened.

Hi, Ross, the Corrective Referee says, turning a spare chair around so he can sit on it backward. I appreciate the effort you're putting into helping Andy out, I really do. It's commendable.

Ross says, He'll snap out of this funk, I know he will. He's a good guy.

For your sake I certainly hope so. You can't expect yourself to maintain your own Performance Parameters if you're doing two monitors' jobs.

He'll get better. I promise.

I know he will, the Corrective Referee says, nodding at one of the monitors. I wouldn't want what happened to that guy to happen to our Andy.

Ross glances at the monitor to see that the subject who fell asleep is clutching his eyes, twisting his body around on the floor in a pool of steaming coffee.

The next morning Andy is already at his station when Ross arrives, busily typing commands into his keyboard. Andy greets Ross warmly and offers him his pastry. Ross feels relieved, happy that his faith in his colleague was correct. They spend the morning talking about entertainments as they perform the functions of their jobs, just like years ago when they began monitoring together.

Sometime after lunch Andy swivels around in his chair excitedly and asks Ross to look at something on one of his monitors. They peer closely at two subjects, except the view has been magnified significantly and they can make out what is on the subjects' monitors.

I finally figured out the secret zoom command, Andy says. See? Just a few keystrokes and I can zoom in even closer.

Ross says nothing, riveted by the image he sees on one of the subject's monitors. He raises his left arm to test his hypothesis and realizes that

it's true. He and Andy are the subjects of these
subjects' monitors.

  When the Corrective Referee arrives with his
assistants in their rubber aprons and gloves, Ross
does not struggle, but Andy does. The referee uses
the eye corer.

II.

They made me watch the procedure. The eye corer
looked like something you might use to drive nails
into a wall, a vibrating, battered machine with a
pistol grip and hoses running to a portable tank
and battery pack. Our Corrective Referee and his
assistants held Andy to the chair and placed the

eyepiece over Andy's face. It didn't take longer than thirty seconds. Once Andy's eyes were removed, they inserted two white ceramic plug-like objects, from the bases of which trailed two cables. Our Corrective Referee plugged these cables into two ports beneath one of Andy's monitors.

How's it looking? our Corrective Referee asked. Is the signal coming through?

Andy nodded.

All good then, our Corrective Referee said as the assistants wiped up some blood with premoistened absorbent wipes.

When they left, I leaned over and whispered, Andy? Are you okay?

Andy nodded.

Andy, I'm so sorry, I said and started to cry. I took hold of his closest hand. It felt cold and drained of blood, probably from the medications they used during the procedure.

Can you see anything? I said.

Yes, Andy said, I can see what's on the monitors. It's like looking down a tunnel at the image. The resolution is better.

In my peripheral vision I spotted a violation and quickly submitted the appropriate alert. Andy groped for his keyboard to log some violations of his own. They were coming in waves subjects falling asleep, defacing their monitors, breaking furniture. Thanks to my quick work, the misbehaving subjects were instantly visited by their

Corrective Referees, who delivered the variety of
punishments they deserved. By the end of my shift
I started hoping something I could barely admit
to myself, that the subjects would violate their
Performance Parameters. I considered the possibility of the subjects wising up and behaving within
their Performance Parameters, and the prospect
oddly disappointed me. The broken fingers and black
eyes that resulted from their disobedience was my
reward for a job performed well.

At the end of our shift, our Corrective Referee
visited to unplug Andy from his monitors and escort
him to his quarters. He gave us both unlimited
entertainment cards. That night I watched three.
One was about a kid who learns how to be cool when

a more popular kid shows him how to dress. Another was a historical entertainment about Vikings. The third was a pornographic entertainment that I'm too ashamed to describe.

The next day Andy arrived before me. He was in a talkative mood.

I can plug these suckers into my ports at home and see the entertainments with crystal clarity, Andy said. Cool, yeah? The Corrective Ref says pretty soon I'll be allowed to hook these things into a video camera so I won't be restricted to just seeing whatever monitor I'm plugged into.

Do they hurt? I said.

They're a little sore, yeah, Andy said. But that's supposed to wear off in a couple days.

I slowly became accustomed to Andy's new way of
monitoring. The more content he seemed with his new
apparatus, the more bored I became. My subjects entered
a long streak of faithfully performing within their
Parameters. I waited with itchy fingers for them to
slip up, to make some fatal error that brought upon
them the wrath of a Corrective Referee, but for the
most part their transgressions were minor. I daydreamed
about a subject smashing a monitor with a chair or
getting up and walking out an hour before his shift
ended. Then I considered an awful thought, some
dark and buoyant fantasy that kept bobbing to the
surface regardless of how I tried to push it down.
I wanted to submit an alert on someone who was
completely innocent, who had not deviated from their

Performance Parameters. With Andy locked into his own personal monitor view, I knew I could probably get away with it. Nobody would see me, not even the hidden others who observed me from miniscule cameras hidden somewhere in the acoustic tile overhead. Whoever was watching me would not be able to discern whether my subjects had in fact deviated from their Performance Parameters. There was a half hour left on my shift. I could simply shelve the idea, go home, eat pizza, and watch some entertainments. Instead I chose my subject randomly and submitted an alert for vandalism.

A couple minutes passed, and I stared at the back of my subject's head. Before him a screen of fuzzed-out, inhuman pixels behaved. The Corrective Referee entered, and I considered submitting an alert correction but knew that alert corrections reflected poorly on one's own performance. The Corrective Referee selected an instrument from his belt and went to work. I could not bear to watch. I had to watch. When the occasion of correction passed, my subject crawled back to his chair and pushed it toward the camera, then climbed onto it so that his face took up nearly the entire monitor. How he knew where to find the camera, I had no idea, but his knowing where it was located seemed to me an admission of his guilt. Then he opened his mouth to show me the bleeding pits where his bottom teeth had been.

At home I vomited for an hour then sat down in my favorite chair to watch an entertainment about a beloved teacher whose unorthodox teaching methods simply aren't understood by the school administration.

The following day I numbly went about my work. I considered submitting a vacation request. My mind wandered to entertainments I had seen, people's faces I had passed in the hallway. Andy hummed and tapped the wrist protector of his keyboard with a pencil in time to a song. Then right before noon all the monitors went blank. Hardware failure. I banged on my monitor with the ball of my hand, but all they displayed was static.

What's going on? Andy said.

Dang monitors blew, I said.

I can see mine just fine, Andy said. What are you seeing?

Nothing, I said.

Must be a connection between the servers and the monitors, Andy said. Hey, it looks like my subjects are having the same problem. I guess this is system-wide.

Can you pull up a Performance Parameter menu? I said.

Yeah, Andy said, hold on a second. I've never had to access this one before. Okay, here. It says that... This can't be correct. "In case of monitor failure, please continue following Performance Parameters and submit alerts on all violations."

But we can't even see our subjects! I said.

It's happening to everyone, Andy said. Oh, Jesus.

I started toward the door. The Corrective Referee and his two assistants met me. On the Corrective Referee's face was an expression of deep, compassionate sadness as he sighed and asked for his tools.

The miner has forgotten the last time he saw daylight. He strikes the earth in front of him, a dim cone of illumination from his helmet reaching precisely as far as the tip of his pick. He clears a space through the rock that frames his body, his ears registering only his breathing and the metronomic blows of his instrument. He loads chunks and dust of rock into the cart behind him and flips the toggle switch to the "Up" position. The cart's battery-powered motor labors as it disappears back through the tunnel he has created, as though it is complaining about the burden he has loaded upon it. The cart returns, each time taking a little longer than last, each time carrying more track and ties that the miner lays down with his hammer, the piercing steel-on-steel ringing no longer making him flinch, and after he lengthens the track he loads it again with rock.

Three times a day the cart bears meals, typically a container of water, bread, beans or rice, a piece of fruit. He eats in the darkness, switching his lamp off, sitting on the wood planks of the bottom of the cart.

He figures he doesn't need to be able to see to eat and that turning the lamp off during meals will make the battery last longer. The cart also delivers, along with his meals, a bucket that he can relieve himself in. It comes with a lid and can be used as a chair.

He has no way to keep track of time, but just as his body seems to be slowing down, the cart arrives with a burlap bag stuffed with straw and a thick wool blanket. He curls his body into the cart and sleeps exactly as long as he needs to, then wakes and resumes his work.

The miner toils but doesn't know it as toiling. It never occurs to him that he could be doing something besides this routine. There is the pick. There is the earth. There is the cart, which trades all that he produces for all that he needs. Pick, earth, cart. He is slowly making one object into smaller objects, which themselves can be made smaller still (he assumes this is what happens to the rocks once they reach the surface). The light before him is no more and no less than the amount of light he needs to see. Time, too, is a substance that he dutifully hacks into components;

the intervals between the sounds of the pick striking rock are segments strung together, composing this thing, his work.

He gathers the rock with his gloved hands and fills the cart. It occurs to him that he could clear the rock faster if he had a shovel, but he's terrified to ask. What if those on the surface denied him his request? The threat of disappointment paralyzes his decision. So he continues stooping over to gather the jagged pieces.

He could ride back up to the surface, he realizes. He could simply climb into the cart, flip the toggle to "Up," and deliver himself from this quiet space deep below the surface. But the thought of riding the cart up makes him shudder more than the thought of asking for a shovel. The arrangement of earth, pick, cart, and miner is too perfect; it is too much what it was intended to be to disturb its equilibrium with the introduction of other elements, namely the surface. The earth, the pick, the cart, and the miner each have their purpose, and in perfectly realizing their purposes seem to blend together, like numbers in an equation pushing ceaselessly toward the single figure on the opposite side of the equal sign. What, then, does this particular equation equal? The miner wonders, asks this question in his head first thing when he wakes, asks it with an inarticulate series of impressions rather than words. The miner senses his irrevocable responsibility to swing the pick at the earth and fill the cart. He sleeps in the cart, which carries all tangible evidence of his work away.

The miner is haunted by the possibility of asking for a shovel and riding the cart to the surface. These are potentialities that he tries to ignore by swinging the pick with more vigor. But when he stops swinging the pick to eat or sleep, these potentialities seem to have regrouped, gathered strength in part of his mind he can't see, their grip on his thoughts more adamant until they come to feel inevitable.

The miner writes "SHOVEL PLEASE" on a paper meal bag, using his finger dipped in spit and dust as a writing instrument. "SHOVEL PLEASE" is the request he sends back to the surface, each word like the arc of his pick—*shovel* the lifting of the pick over his head, *please* the striking of the earth. He chants the words in his head as he works. Shovel *please*. Shovel *please*. Their meaning evaporates.

When the cart returns there is no shovel, only a meal, his refuse bucket, and more track to lay. He wants to smash the cart with his pick, but his strength disappears, forced out of him by the magnitude of his disappointment, and he simply sits in the cart in the dark trying to eat while crying. It is hard because he is so hungry, yet the food keeps falling from his mouth as he sobs. When he has finished crying and eating he continues his work of laying the track and striking the earth with his pick, gathering the rocks with his hands and dumping them in the cart.

When his mat and blanket come he lies speculating about why his request was not met. Perhaps those on the surface are callous. Perhaps his work is punishment for something he can't remember having done. Or maybe they didn't see the note or were unable to read it. His request for the shovel wasn't met not because they are cruel, then, but because he made some kind of mistake, perhaps even made the mistake of requesting the shovel to begin with.

The miner then is seized by the terrible thought that perhaps he had to make his request in person. He works three cycles, his hands aching as they yearn for the shovel, until he can stand it no longer, then climbs into the cart, flips the switch to the "Up" position and feels the cart start to move. He barrels through the blackness on the tracks he laid, his stomach growing hungrier, his lamp illuminating nothing less than the inability to see anything. He sleeps three times, and wakes after the third time to find the cart has come to a halt.

The miner climbs out of the cart, finds where the tracks end, and turns to face a wall of earth as solid as the one he left. Has he ended up where he started? He quickly rules out that possibility, as the toggle switch is now on the side of the cart furthest from this wall. This tunnel has no exit.

The miner buries his face in his hands and weeps. When his eyes stop, he rides back to his starting point, sweeping the lamp from side to side to see if perhaps he had passed a juncture somewhere, but he had not. The tunnel has no branches. It is a single hollow passage within the earth.

Overwhelmed by hunger, the miner tries to work after he sends the cart away, hoping it will return soon with a meal. He swings the pick, embarrassed he ever asked for a shovel. His chant of "shovel *please* shovel *please*" turns into a taunt. The cart returns with a meal that he eats greedily, licking his fingers and almost choking on pieces of bread he forgets to chew.

Then he works. He swings the pick and strikes the earth with renewed energy, converting the anger and shame of his request for something to alleviate his burden into more loads of rock. He sleeps when the cart brings him his bed, eats when it brings him his food, lays the rails and ties for miles through this dense, perfect geology.

The miner raises his pick, brings it down, and strikes light. Just a pinprick at first, then a shaft of illumination that grows in circumference and contour the more he strikes. He closes his eyes, striking blindly as a cold wind rushes into the passage. All is pure white light. No object within view has shape or definition in his overwhelmed eyes.

Panting, he lets his pick fall to the ground and kneels at the portal roughly the size of his body, waiting for something, hands covering his face from a sun that seems to come from every direction. This is the surface.

The miner shuts his eyes and falls asleep in the cart, and if an interval of night passes, he sleeps through it. When he awakens he finds himself surrounded by light as painfully bright as before. He wants someone to appear and give him directions on how to proceed, but no one comes. He grows restless and hungry. If no one comes to tell him what to do, he might as well return to the opposite end of the tunnel to continue his work. The prospect of returning to his duties cheers him, and after wrestling with his thoughts a moment, he gathers his tools and sets out for the furthest reaches of his private darkness.

The

AUTHOR OF THIS BOOK WOULD LIKE TO THANK

THE BOUDINOTS
LEAH BROCK
DAVE CORNELIUS

AND

THE EDITORS OF THE JOURNALS IN WHICH THESE STORIES FIRST APPEARED

Ryan Boudinot is the author of the novels *Blueprints of the Afterlife* and *Misconception* and the story collection *The Littlest Hitler*.

He is the founder of Seattle City of Literature.
For more information, visit seattlecityoflit.org.

EDITOR AND ASSOCIATE PUBLISHER: Eric Reynolds
BOOK DESIGNER: Jacob Covey
COPYEDITOR: Janice Lee
PUBLISHER: Gary Groth

FANTAGRAPHICS BOOKS

Seattle, Washington, USA

Library of Congress Control Number: 2015932756
ISBN 978-1-60699-847-2
Printed in China

"Death by Tchotchke" appeared in *We Are the Friction*; "The End of Bert and Ernie" appeared in *Golden Handcuffs Review*; "Robot Sex" appeared in *McSweeney's*; "An Essay and a Story about Mötley Crüe" appeared in *Opium* and was anthologized in *Blurring the Boundaries: Explorations to the Fringes of Nonfiction*; "Chopsticks" appeared in *Monkeybicycle*; "The Armies of Elfland" appeared in *The Lifted Brow*; "Cardiology" appeared on Five Chapters and was anthologized in *Real Unreal: Best American Fantasy* and *Best Bizarro Fiction of the Decade*; "The Guy Who Kept Meeting Himself" appeared in *McSweeney's*; "Readers & Writers" appeared in *Post Road*; "Monitors" appeared in *Booth*; "The Mine" appeared in *Monkeybicycle*.

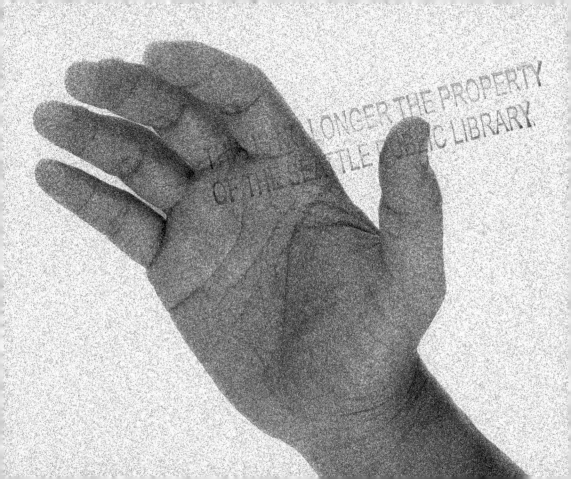